OTHER WORLDLY HOLIDAYS

ANTHOLOGY TWO

CONNIE SUTTLE

Print ISBN: 1-63478-082-5
Print ISBN-13: 978-163478-082-7
2nd Edition eBook ISBN: 1-63478-081-7
2nd Edition eBook ISBN-13: 978-1-63478-081-0

Published by:
SubtleDemon Publishing, LLC
PO Box 95696
Oklahoma City, OK 73143

Cover art by Renee Barratt @ The Cover Counts

To Walter, Joe, Larry, Lee, Dianne, Sarah and Mark.
Thank you.

ACKNOWLEDGMENTS

As always, this book is the result of collaboration. If it weren't for the support of my editor, my cover artist and my beta readers, it would be less than it is. All mistakes, as usual, are mine and no other's.

About the Author:
Connie Suttle lives in Oklahoma with her husband and a conglomerate of cats. They have finally banded together to make their demands, which has proven disconcerting to all humans involved.

You may find Connie in the following ways:
Facebook: Connie Suttle Author
Twitter: @subtledemon
Website and Blog: subtledemon.com

ALSO BY CONNIE SUTTLE

Blood Destiny Series[1]

Blood Wager

Blood Passage

Blood Sense

Blood Domination

Blood Royal

Blood Queen

Blood Rebellion

Blood War

Blood Redemption

Blood Reunion

Blood Recall

Blood Alliance

Legend of the Ir'Indicti Series[1]

Bumble

Shadowed

Target

Vendetta

Destroyer

High Demon Series[1]

Demon Lost

Demon Revealed

Demon's King

Demon's Quest

Demon's Revenge

Demon's Dream

God Wars Series[1]

Blood Double

Blood Trouble

Blood Revolution

Blood Love

Blood Finale

Saa Thalarr Series

Hope and Vengeance

Wyvern and Company

Observe and Protect[2]

First Ordinance Series[1]

Finder

Keeper

BlackWing

SpellBreaker

WhiteWing

R-D Series[1]

Cloud Dust

Cloud Invasion

Cloud Rebel

Latter Day Demons Series[1]

Hot Demon in the City

A Demon's Work is Never Done

A Demon's Due

Seattle Elementals Series

Your Money's Worth

Worth Your While[2]

BlackWing Pirates Series

MindSighted

MindMage

MindRogue

MindMaster[2]

Black Rose Sorceress Series[1]

The Rose Mark

Rose and Thorn

Black Rose Queen

Queen of Thorns and Roses

Future Wars Series
Buffer Zone
Black Zone[2]

Anthologies
Other Worldly Ways
Other Worldly Holidays

Other Titles from SubtleDemon Publishing:
Ren Gifford Mysteries
Malefactor
Transgressor
Underhanded[2]
by Joe Scholes

[1]Indicates this series is available as a Boxed Set in e-book format.
[2]Forthcoming

CONTENTS

GSW, OR HOW I MET MY MOTHER

Chapter 1   3

QUEEN'S HOLIDAY

Chapter 1   29
Chapter 2   40
Chapter 3   47
Chapter 4   57
Chapter 5   64
Chapter 6   72

ROSE OF THE PEAKS

Chapter 1   77
Chapter 2   92
Chapter 3   106

GSW, OR HOW I MET MY MOTHER

*I*f I hadn't shot myself in the foot (in the physical sense) with my dumb-ass husband's gun the day before New Year's Eve, I wouldn't have been sitting on an examination table in the hospital emergency room, talking to the suicide who'd died five minutes before I arrived.

He was seventeen and too talkative for a suicide, I decided, when he tried to show me the exit wound in his head. Spirits don't have exit wounds, or any other wounds showing after they die but I didn't want to point out the obvious to him. He saw me as a kindred spirit, albeit a live one, since I'd also shot myself.

"Mine was an accident," I told him for the third time. I glanced behind him, through the door to my cubicle. A nurse walked past, shaking her head as her soft-soled shoes squeaked on tiles smelling of disinfectant. The nurse thought I was talking to myself, since she couldn't see or hear spirits. Just what I needed, somebody thinking I had a bigger dose of crazy than I already did. My left foot throbbed where I'd shot it; I'd wrapped it in a kitchen towel and could only find duct tape to secure it to my foot before driving myself to the hospital. I'd called my best friend and next-door neighbor Shane Taylor, but he'd been in a meeting. He served on the committee that planned a charity ball every year for aids patient.

"Why did you have a gun, then, if you didn't intend to—you know?" Suicide attempted to get my attention again.

"People handle guns all the time without intending to off themselves," I said absently, glancing at the Williams and Sonoma kitchen towel that wrapped my foot. Red seeped around edges of hastily wrapped duct tape, and I figured I'd have to buy another towel.

"In my case," I continued, "My idiot husband was cleaning his .22 pistol last night, until a client called and he never put it back in the safe where it usually stays. I picked it up to put it away this morning when something startled me. I dropped the gun and shot my foot."

"The docs aren't gonna believe that story," Suicide offered a lopsided grin. He hadn't been awful looking when he was alive, even if he did have ears that belonged on a larger head. I might have asked

3

him what his story was if I had more time and wasn't bleeding into a kitchen towel, all while medical personnel listened in to see if I didn't need a psych consult in addition to emergency wound care.

"Look," I said to Suicide Boy, "If you can't find your way over, I can take you later. Right now, I have my own fish to fry."

I've lived in Atlanta all my life, and I'm proud of my roots. If I have a bit of a drawl, along with plenty of southern euphemisms, I come by them honestly.

Suicide was searching for an appropriate comment when Shane rushed in, an emergency room intern right behind him. "Conner, darlin', what the hell happened?" Shane demanded.

"Steven forgot to put his gun away last night. He was cleaning it and left it on the coffee table in the den when he got up to answer the phone, so I picked it up to put it away this morning. That damn cat that's roaming the neighborhood managed to get in the house and scared the hell out of me. I dropped the gun and shot myself in the foot."

I'd said this in a rush, so Suicide wouldn't jump in on the conversation and distract me. Shane gave my towel and duct tape covered foot a critical and disapproving stare. So did the intern. In fact, Intern had an eyebrow lifted so high I figured he might need therapy to talk it down again. He stuck his head out the door and yelled for a nurse and a suture tray.

"Shane," I mumbled, "we have a visitor." I jerked my head toward Suicide Boy.

"Well, what do you expect? This is a hospital," Shane put his hands on his hips and stated the obvious at the same time. Shane can't see spirits, but he and my son Steve Jr. are the only people who truly believe I can see them. Oh, and perhaps the dozens of people I've been compelled to deliver messages to over the years. Sometimes they believe me. Sometimes.

A nurse walked in with a mound of wrapped medical supplies shoved into a pink plastic tub. She hauled a tray table over, plopped the tub on it and proceeded to lay things out. Intern grabbed the scissors and then examined my foot, first this way and then that, trying, I'm sure, to figure out the best way to cut into my towel and duct tape. "A cat, huh?" Intern asked as he made the first cut.

"A more devious and felonious feline you might never hope to meet," I nodded, wincing as he jerked on my towel while snipping. "I'm thinking about pressing charges."

"Conner, I told you to call animal control, but of course you ignored me," Shane wore his finest, longest-suffering, I'm your best friend but only because I'm a saint expression.

"They'd kill it," I muttered. "He's not the best lookin' cat I've ever seen. People don't adopt animals like that."

"Conner Louella Francis, have you been feeding that stray behind my back?" Shane's elbows went up a notch, and indignation wasn't far behind them.

"He likes leftover tuna," I mumbled, attempting to defend myself.

"Conner, you're a vegetarian and Steven hates tuna." Shane wanted to swear, I could tell, but his southern upbringing came into play and he didn't. Not in front of strangers, anyway. "You've been buying tuna to feed that cat, he gets in the house and now you have a hole in your foot."

"Mrs. Francis, you know we had to call the police since this is a gunshot wound," Intern said as he removed the towel from my foot. He dumped my sixteen-dollar kitchen towel into a wastebasket, (I wasn't worried about the loss of the duct tape—that was Steven's) and examined the hole in my foot with glove-covered efficiency. It still seeped blood and Suicide leaned in to examine it. Shane moved closer at the same time and he and Suicide occupied the same space for a brief moment. That always makes me nauseated, so the nurse had to shove the pink tub into my lap as my breakfast came up with eye-popping momentum.

The intern backed away quickly; I'm sure he didn't want to pull bits of scrambled egg from his hair after tending my injury, but I managed to hit the tub. Mostly. The police walked in right as I was coughing up cranberry juice. I'm sure that presented a pleasant image to the two officers, who now stood inside the door of my cubicle. One had the decency to turn his head. I hate for somebody to watch me throw up—it's embarrassing. I don't ever ask anybody to hold my hair when I puke.

Suicide stepped away as the officers walked in, and the room got crowded as another nurse entered the room. I recognized her as the one who'd heard me talking to Suicide a few moments before. She had another doctor with her. He wore glasses over weak hazel eyes and that, coupled with thinning brown hair and a white coat pronounced him to be the resident shrink. And then, to complicate things further, another spirit followed right behind Shrink and the nurse.

Suicide knew somehow that the new spirit was somebody he could speak to and sidled up to him immediately. "So, how did you croak?" he asked the new arrival.

The nurse took the tub away after she determined I was finished puking, the intern cautiously approached my foot again and one of the officers stepped forward with a form in his hand. Shane backed against the cubicle wall and Suicide traded causes of death with the new spirit. Shrink took in my appearance with an objective and clinical stare.

"So, Mrs. uh, Francis," the form-bearing officer asked after checking the name on the paper he held, "You say you shot yourself in the foot?"

"Yes," I replied, almost jerking my foot away from the intern's hands. He'd hit a tender spot. "I thought about putting the foot in my mouth instead, but I'm not as flexible as I once was."

"How did this happen?" the second officer asked, ignoring my attempt at humor.

"Husband, gun, phone call, cat," I itemized the list of causes on my fingers.

"Your husband shot you?" The officer studied me with procedural curiosity.

"Oh for heaven's sake, no," I said. "Not that I wouldn't mind sending Steven's mail to a prison address, but he was at work when this happened. It should all be there on that paper you're waving around," I pointed at the form the first officer held.

"You shot yourself because you have anger issues with your

husband?" Shrink now spoke up. He had a slight paunch to go with the thinning hair and weak eyesight, and if he hadn't started digging at me, I might have harbored some sympathy for him.

"I have anger issues, all right, but they don't include physical pain or bullet holes on my person," I snapped. Shane made a slashing motion with his hand, silently begging me to shut up. Shrink saw this and a light appeared in his eyes. Shrink was either having a religious experience or thinking that I was plotting my husband's death with Shane as an accomplice. Possibly both. How was I to know?

"Look," I said, "I accidentally shot myself. My husband left his gun out, I picked it up to put it away this morning, the cat ran through and startled me, I dropped the gun, it went off and the bullet went through my foot. I was not plotting the demise of my husband, the cat or my foot. It was an accident."

Suicide and his new BFF came over, walking through one of the officers to do it. I almost went into dry heaves again, but managed to keep my gag reflex under control this time.

"You think they're gonna put you in the psych ward?" Suicide asked. "I've been there a couple of times. I can give you pointers."

"I'll bet you can," I said aloud without thinking. Who knew that a hole in my foot would allow all my good sense to leak out?

"She can see us?" BFF was now very interested in me. "Can you tell my wife she's a cheating whore and I knew she was fooling around with Steve?"

"Steve who?" I opened my mouth again; I couldn't help it. I swear, if he said Steven Francis, I planned to start screaming right there in the emergency room. No, I didn't think my Steven had screwed every woman in Atlanta. From a logical standpoint he hadn't had time to get to all of them yet.

"Steve Emerlin," BFF said. I breathed a relived sigh, then jumped when I realized that Shrinkman was now standing at my side, half in and half out of Suicide. He'd had to move the cops aside to get there. I wondered when he'd whip out that cell phone or whatever it was he had clipped to his belt and call for the straitjacket. Queasiness tried to win out, again, and I couldn't help it, I reached out and nudged

Shrinkman to the left, separating him from Suicide. I could hear his little hardwired brain adding obsessive-compulsive to his list of other diagnoses.

"Are you gonna tell my wife or not?" BFF demanded, coming to stand next to Suicide. The intern was cleaning the bullet hole with a squirt bottle filled with fluid, and I almost kicked him in the face, I was so surprised. It wasn't the most pleasant experience I'd ever had, either.

"Where is she?" I gasped, attempting to keep my unruly foot under control.

"Down the hall," BFF said.

"Her name?"

"Conner," Shane whispered from his spot against the wall. His voice held a warning, but he knew when a spirit asked to have a message delivered, it did become an obsession. I didn't eat or sleep well until I'd made the delivery—or the best attempt I could.

"Sandra Broom," BFF replied, ignoring Shane.

"Shane, go down the hall and get Sandra Broom," I sighed, then almost pulled my foot out of intern's grasp; he was attempting to give me local anesthetic and, I admit, I don't much like needles.

"I'll deliver the message, but I'll be nicer about it," I gasped to BFF as the needle went into my foot.

"I'll take what I can get," BFF nodded his acceptance. Shrinkman was having a field day, I could tell. He was smiling and ticking off "delusional" on his mental list.

The two officers had now backed against the wall and were watching all this with interest. I guess their normal, everyday lives didn't include this brand of lunacy. Shane came in a few minutes later with a woman I assumed was Sandra Broom, and there was a man with her.

"Steve, I presume?" I nodded toward the man, and BFF nodded in return. I cleared my throat. "Sandra," I began, "Your husband, uh, what's your name, honey?" I asked BFF.

"Andy," he told me.

"Uh, Andy here tells me that he was completely, unequivocally and

8

in all other ways knowledgeable about you and Steve." Her eyes grew round.

"How?" she whispered, a shaking hand at her throat.

"Um," Andy said. I think if he could have, he'd have turned red. He shuffled non-existent feet instead.

"Fess up," I told him. I wasn't about to let him off the hook, especially since this was going to land me in a locked ward where I'd be forced to answer questions about my mother. Shrinkman was becoming positively gleeful.

"Her panties," Andy muttered. He looked to be in his twenties, but all spirits look young and healthy to me. Sandra, on the other hand, looked to be in her forties. I figured Andy had to be around the same age.

"What about her panties?" I demanded. All right, I was lightheaded. Under normal circumstances, I don't think I would ever say the word *panties* in mixed company. Unless I knew the mixed company in the biblical sense, that is.

"I, uh, like the scent," Andy admitted. I thought he was going to phase out, right then and there.

"Oh, no you don't," I almost yelled at him. "I'll tell her, but by damn you're gonna stay here and face the consequences. You asked for this, remember?" I turned back to Sandra. "He liked the scent of your underwear, and he, uh," I couldn't go farther than that—it was too embarrassing. Sandra got the message, though. She turned a bright enough red to do for her and Andy both. She buried her head in her hands.

"Happy now?" I asked Andy. He hung his head.

"I loved her," he said unhappily. "That was the worst day of my life."

"He says he loved you and that was the worst day of his life," I told Sandra. She looked up, and there were tears in her eyes.

"I love you, too, Andy," Sandra said before rushing from the room. Cheatin' Steve followed close behind. Andy stood there with his ghostly mouth hanging open for a moment before phasing out. He'd found his way over, at least. Suicide was now looking at me with interest.

"Don't you be getting any ideas," I told him, looking down to see the intern dragging sutures through my skin. I shouldn't have looked. I turned my head and almost bumped into Shrinkman, he was standing so close.

"You can speak with spirits," he said. I had a vision of him rubbing his hands together, anxious to start a battery of tests that no normal person would ever want to undergo. Well, no abnormal person either, and I was sure I fell somewhere in the latter category.

"Look," I said. "You and I don't need to have quiet bedside chats while I attempt to escape my restraints. Run along, now. I hear your mother calling."

Shrinkman almost jumped when I said that. "She's here?" He asked, turning frantically and looking about him. All right, that was downright spooky. Fortuitous, but spooky.

"Hey, maybe I should buy the doc here a cup of coffee." Shane attempted to rescue me from my current predicament. I didn't know if it would work—not this late in the game. Shane steered Shrinkman out of the room. Suicide came back and stood in his place. Both cops were still there and still listening. "What's your name?" I asked Suicide. What the hell? I was already getting a reservation for a rubber room.

"Sam Melton," he replied with an embarrassed shrug.

"Sam Melton? Mayor's son Sam Melton?" I couldn't believe what I was hearing.

"Yeah. The old man doesn't know yet," Sam grinned sheepishly.

"Oh, good grief," I said. Both cops had come to stand beside my exam table, and they were almost melding with Sam. Intern stitched up the last of my bullet wound.

"What's this about Sam Melton?" Cop One asked.

"He's dead, self-inflicted bullet wound," I told them.

"Nobody knows that, we're keeping it under wraps until the Mayor gets here," Cop Two informed me.

"Sam knows," I said. "He tells me he fired the gun into his left temple, and the bullet exited from the right."

"Tell them I was in the basement, not far from the water heater,"

Sam grinned. I had never seen anyone so happy about the circumstances of their death before.

"He says he was in the basement, near the water heater," I told both officers.

"Uncle Ed was there, too. I shot him, first," Sam smiled.

"Oh my gosh, he says he shot his Uncle Ed, first," I told the cops. They were now gaping at each other.

"That bastard won't ever touch me or my sister again," Sam said happily. "He threatened us. He said he had something on dad, and he'd tell and ruin him if we said anything."

"Officers, you'd better interview Sam's sister. Sam says that they were both molested by Uncle Ed." I looked down at the intern, who was now staring—hard—at me. He'd finished sewing and now held my foot in his hand. The nurse, who also had a stunned look on her face, absently handed a roll of gauze off to the intern. He shook himself out of his temporary shock and started wrapping my foot. One of the officers got on his radio and relayed the message.

"I'd appreciate it if you boys would leave my name out of all this," I said. "I promise not to come near the hospital again, ever, if I can help it."

Cop One nodded, said something else into his radio when it squawked back and he and Cop Two took off at a run out the door. Intern finished bandaging my foot, wrote a prescription for pain meds and left, shaking his head. The nurse was afraid to leave but she had to; she needed a wheelchair to get me down the hall so I could check out and go home.

"Very nice," a tall, blue man appeared at my side. I looked up, then looked up some more. "I'll be taking this information back with me," he said. "And you won't be able to mention me to anyone."

"Why in heaven's name would I want to?" I asked, staring rudely. I mean, how many times can you say a tall blue man visited me in the hospital emergency room before everybody thinks you're certifiable? "You think I want them to know I'm crazy?"

"You're not crazy," he informed me, crossing long blue arms over his chest. He looked like a hippie, if hippies were nine feet tall and blue-skinned. Loose weave natural fabrics, sewn into a hip-length tunic and loose pants were what he wore, and he was barefoot. "I'm sorry I startled you this morning. I allowed the cat inside. I didn't realize you might drop the weapon. The animal was hungry and I was only watching you, I promise. My kind means no harm."

"All right, maybe I need that rubber room after all," I muttered. "Or I'm hallucinating."

"Neither," he assured me. "Would you like for me to follow you home?"

"Can you drive?" I asked. "My car is in the parking lot."

"I have never attempted to operate a vehicle, before. It would be a new experience." He looked as if that might be something he'd enjoy trying.

"Look," I said, "If you don't have a license, you won't be driving. That voids my insurance." I deliberately didn't mention that he'd never fit inside my car, as tall as he was.

"I have no need for a license," he said, and watched as the nurse rolled a wheelchair in the room. She acted as if she didn't see the blue man, and I sure as hell wasn't about to draw her attention to that fact. I wanted to go home, take my pain medication and crawl into bed. Maybe Shane's sympathy would kick in and he'd bring me soup.

The nurse took me down to the desk after she handed off a pile of papers telling me how to take care of my wound and not to get it wet when I bathed. I blew out a sigh and resigned myself to the fact that I wouldn't be getting in the hot tub for a while.

Blue man strolled casually beside me, as if he did that sort of thing every day, I got copies of the release forms, paid my co-pay and the nurse pushed me toward the sliding doors that led into the emergency room. I started to ask the nurse where she thought she was taking me; they'd already told me I shouldn't be driving, but she just went right along, left the wheelchair outside the doors, then turned and went back inside. I looked up at my tall blue escort. "Now what?" I asked.

"I will drive you home," he said, and did something, I'm not sure what, that made him around three feet shorter and human looking. He still had blond hair, which looked nice, actually.

"You just told me you didn't drive and don't have a license," I reminded him. He grinned at me, lifted me from the wheelchair like I weighed five pounds and carried me to my car. It was then I realized that I'd locked my keys inside. I said a few of my choicest cuss words then, but formerly blue and tall didn't seem to mind.

It also didn't matter that I'd locked myself out of the car. He just put a finger to the handle, I heard the lock click and he opened the door. He deposited me on the passenger seat, then climbed in on the driver's side. I briefly wondered where Shane was and if he were still trying to pull Shrinkman's focus away from me.

"Do not fear, all will be well," my unlicensed companion informed me and turned the key in the ignition, starting the car. He put it in gear, backed out of the space carefully and pointed it in the right direction to go home. I leaned back and kept my mouth shut. He drove quite well and never exceeded the speed limit. I heaved a big sigh when we pulled into the driveway and parked.

"You have so driven before," I accused as he came around and opened my door, again lifting and carrying me. We got inside the house and he turned back to his natural blue self once we were there.

"That was excellent, I may have to attempt driving again," he informed me with a satisfied grin and set me down on the kitchen island. I watched as he rummaged through the refrigerator for something, eventually coming out with a premixed protein drink. I usually kept some on hand, for emergencies. 'Here," he handed it to me. I must have been giving him a puzzled look because he took it back, popped it open without touching the lid and handed it back to me. "Drink," he commanded. I drank.

"I need my pain medication," I told him as I sucked up my drink. He snorted at my announcement and took my foot in his hands. Light shone around his fingers and the pain disappeared, just like that.

"What did you do?" I asked breathlessly.

"That is simple to fix," he said.

"Hi." Sam Melton appeared in my kitchen.

"Sam, I thought you'd gone on," my voice sounded whiny, even to my own ears. Here was trouble, back again. I don't do well with spirits if I'm sick.

"Nope. I went to check on those officers. They were telling somebody to go question sis," he went to the fridge and attempted to open the door. Finding that his hand went right through it, he stuck his head inside it instead, to check out the contents. "Why don't you have any soda?" he asked, pulling his head out again and handing me a disappointed look.

"Sam, you gave up sodas when you picked up that gun," I said. "Why didn't you talk to your father about what was going on? I think you loved him, maybe."

"Dad was always so busy," Sam said. "Are you sure I can't eat or drink anything?" I looked over at blue man and rolled my eyes.

"I can't see him or hear him," blue man said.

"Oh good gosh," I said. "And what's your name, anyway, so I don't have to think of you as blue guy all the time."

Sam was now staring at the blue guy, as if he hadn't noticed him until that moment. "My name is Garegar," blue guy said. He'd pronounced it Gary-gar. "I am Larentii," he added, as if that meant anything to me.

"Well, Garegar, my husband will be home in about an hour. If he finds you here, he may have an aneurysm. Not that it's a bad thing," I told him, holding out a hand. "I'm just warning you."

"He will not be able to see me unless I wish it, and I will not wish it," Garegar informed me.

"From what you said earlier, sounds like your husband's lyin' and cheatin'," Sam observed, walking around my kitchen to check everything out.

"Oh, he's cheatin', all right," I said. "But he doesn't lie about it. He'd tell me right to my face if I asked him. He'd probably laugh about it, too, while he was at it."

"Then why do you stay with him? Is it this fancy house and the money?" Sam asked, looking around my kitchen in appreciation.

"Well, not because it's his fancy house and money," I grumbled. "It's all mine, I inherited it from my mother," I said. "We didn't sign a prenup when we married, and we married young. Now, we don't sleep in the same bedroom, he only speaks when he wants something and he's threatened to ruin me if I ask for a divorce."

"How can he ruin you?" Sam blinked at me.

"Sam, not everybody can see ghosts," I muttered. Steven could ruin me and my career if he wanted. All he'd have to do is talk to a few reporters and Conner Francis would be virtual toast.

We all whirled at the sound of the key turning in the back door, but it was only Shane. Rain was falling now; Shane shook water from his curly brown hair when he came through the door. Shane has had a key to the house since day one, almost, and he knows if anything ever happens to me to have Steven investigated first.

"Conner, how the hell did you get home?" he asked. "Your car's parked out front. Tell me you didn't drive."

"I didn't drive," I said.

"Then how did you get home?" he demanded. I swear, sometimes he was worse than a mother hen. A gay mother hen, but still.

"Someone drove me," I said.

"Someone I know?" he was giving me the eye, telling me silently that I better not have let a stranger drive me home. I didn't want to get into it with Shane; not with Sam and Garegar there to watch.

"We have visitors," I nodded toward Sam and Garegar.

"So what?" Shane was about to get warmed up. "You did, didn't you. You let a stranger drive you home. Conner, do you understand how dangerous that is? I swear, those cupcakes you hide in your desk drawer are warping your brain. That, and the fact that you stay up all night writing."

I didn't have a defense against anything he said. I didn't know why I'd gone with Garegar and let him drive. I couldn't explain it. He just seemed safe, somehow. And I did stay up writing until all hours of the night. I'd been publishing books under a pen name for years, mysteries with a Southern female sleuth. Cozies, they called them. That didn't mean I was just going to sit there and take the truth lying down.

"Shane Patrick Taylor, get off my ass," I said. "I've had an awful day, that shrink probably still wants to lock me up, Sam's still here and Steven will likely be here any minute, wondering where his dinner is."

"Where's that gun? I may shoot Steven myself," Shane declared.

"Come on," I said, sliding off the island. "Help me throw something together." Shane could cook as well as I could; better at times. He made the best barbecue in Atlanta, and when he had a cookout, everybody came, including people he didn't invite. Even our homophobic neighbors forgave Shane for his transgressions, as they called them, on the days he served up ribs and brisket.

Steven had stuffed pork chops waiting on him when he arrived, and he didn't say a word to me or notice my wrapped foot, which I preferred, by the way, stuffed himself, then went to his study. Garegar and Sam watched Shane and me the whole time we put the meal together, then watched as Steven consumed it. Shane helped me get the dishes into the dishwasher afterward, then went out the back door and through the connecting gate in our mutual fence to go home.

I sighed and went toward my study. It's on the second floor of my home, just down the hall from my bedroom. Steven sleeps in the master suite downstairs. I don't mind. I don't have to see him after dinner, most days. Garegar and Sam followed along behind me. Garegar must have gotten impatient while I hobbled up the stairs one step at a time, because he picked me up again and carried me to my bedroom. We went right past my study, even though I protested when he walked by.

"You will sleep," he said, laying me on the bed. I started to climb right off again to walk down the hall to my study, but he poked my forehead with a long blue finger and I didn't remember anything else after that.

I woke on New Year's Eve to the doorbell ringing, so I slid off the bed and hobbled around looking for my robe. I wouldn't have bothered, normally; Shane would let himself in and Gayle, my neighbor on the other side, knew to call first. I was expecting a last minute delivery—

advance copies of my latest novel from the publisher and I was afraid it was Fed-Ex at the door.

I stubbed the toe of my bullet-hole-riddled foot on the corner of the bed, howled in pain and dropped to the floor trying to hug my foot to me. Trust me, when you get to be fifty-three (unless you're a yoga instructor), that's easier said than done. I had tears of pain in my eyes and felt truly sorry for myself when Garegar appeared in the bedroom with my package in his hand.

"Thanks," I sniffled as he handed the box to me. I blinked up at him. Frankly, I was hoping he'd been a hallucination and would be gone today. I forgave him for being an uninvited houseguest, however, since he'd answered the door for me. And he knelt in the floor and fixed my foot again. Anybody who could do that was welcome in my home for at least a one-week stay and regular meals.

That brought back my Southern manners, which had been noticeable absent the day before. "Are you hungry?" I asked, staring into his bright-blue eyes. I figured I could at least cook breakfast for him.

"I do not consume food as the humanoid races do," he informed me. He took my hand and pulled me to my feet. "We feed directly from a source of energy. Sunlight is our usual sustenance."

"Well, that might cut out a few trips to the store," I muttered, staring down at the foot he'd just fixed. I discovered I was dressed in an old blue nightgown I hadn't worn for months. I didn't remember putting it on, either. Casting an accusing glare at my guest, I gave an indignant "What the hell?" Garegar realized his welcome had just evaporated.

"My apologies," he sighed. "I felt obligated to determine which sleeping garment you might wish to be dressed in, and since that one showed the most signs of wear, I assumed it must be your favorite."

I stared up at my houseguest and blew a stray strand of hair off my face. "It isn't your logic I have a problem with," I snapped.

"I hear your race has an irrational fear of nudity," he replied, rubbing my shoulders gently with a large blue hand. "We Larentii regard nudity as perfectly natural. Clothing should be worn for protective purposes only, or to prevent offense."

"Well, let's discuss that offense thing, then," I shook a finger at him. I didn't get a chance to tell him what else was on my mind because the doorbell rang again. I looked around for the robe I hadn't found the first time. I cursed creatively when I didn't find it. Garegar did something with his hand, and the robe was just there.

"Thanks," I said ungratefully and hobbled out the door. I was heading toward the stairs and shrugging into my robe as I did so. Who says I can't multitask? Garegar must have sensed that I wasn't in the mood for any more of his help right then and merely watched me struggle down the stairs, following along behind patiently. I flung the front door open when I finally reached it, and wished I hadn't bothered once I saw who it was. It was Shrinkman, whose name I hadn't gotten the day before.

"Go away," I snapped unkindly. I know, that's exactly the opposite of what my Southern upbringing had taught me to do, but there wasn't any way I wanted to see this guy, much less offer him sweet iced tea and cookies. I thought about slamming the door in his face, but my mother would have wept to see me behave that way, so I didn't.

"Mrs. Francis, please," Shrinkman begged me to allow him inside the house.

"Look, I'm not sitting on your couch and answering a bunch of questions. I don't have time for that." He was disappointed; his watery hazel eyes stared at me mournfully through designer spectacles.

Garegar was still standing beside me, but Shrinkman had no clue. "I'm begging you, Mrs. Francis," Shrinkman said. He really was begging. He sounded desperate. "I don't want you to answer questions, exactly. I want you to ask my mother to go on and stop haunting me."

"Your mother? Where is she?" I asked, looking around him. There weren't any spirits visible.

"She's right here, nagging," Shrinkman said, nodding to the left. That would have put her in my ornamental Japanese shrubbery, but I didn't point that out.

"Honey, are you sure?" I asked. All right, my sympathy and my Southern roots had just reappeared. Go ahead; call me an idiot.

"She's here," Shrinkman insisted.

I turned my head and looked up at Garegar, who gave me a human-influenced shrug. I turned back to Shrinkman. "All right, honey, what's your name? Shane gets upset if I allow strangers into my home."

"Shane's the one who invited me for coffee yesterday?"

"Yes. That was Shane. What's your name?"

"Melford—Melford Mitchell," he said. Well, I was really feeling sorry for him, now. With a name like Melford, he had to be scarred for life. That was half his problem, right there.

"So, uh, Doctor Mitchell, then," I said. I couldn't bring myself to say Melford. He nodded enthusiastically. "Doctor Mitchell, please come in and have some tea." He walked through the door and I was about to close it when the police cruiser drove up. "Oh lord," I muttered to myself when the two officers from yesterday's visit to the emergency room climbed out of the car. Doctor Mitchell was now peering over my shoulder at my newly arrived guests, but it wasn't over, yet. A Cadillac Limo pulled in right behind the cruiser and the Mayor, his driver and his bodyguard got out.

I gazed helplessly at Garegar; he was now the only one in the room with whom I could be honest. My life had gone from calm to complicated in the time it takes rabbits to reproduce. Garegar shrugged again. Sighing heavily and plastering a smile on my face, I turned to greet my new guests.

We ended up at the island in the kitchen; I served glasses of iced tea and cookies that I'd shaken out of boxes and onto plates. Invited guests got homemade. You show up unexpected, you get boxed. That's just the way it works.

"Now," I said, as cheerfully as I could manage. I mean, really, the Mayor was in mourning. What do you do about that? Sam, whom I was hoping had found his way over, had come in with his father and was hovering. I knew that look he wore—guilt. Now that the deed was done and he was seeing how much suffering had actually occurred as a result, well, there you go.

Everybody seemed to be waiting for the Mayor to speak; he was the ranking official in my kitchen right then. He appeared to be having trouble gathering his thoughts. "I heard you talked to Sam," he said, choking up on the words.

Oh, I felt sympathy for him, all right. I couldn't even imagine what place I'd be in if Steve Jr. was dead. He was in special ops in the military, so that was a constant worry. "Yes, I talked to Sam yesterday," I managed to say to the Mayor. "I think he loves you." Sam looked up at my words.

"I do love you, Dad," Sam said. He was trying to put his arms around his father, but it wasn't working out very well. The embrace went right through his father's body. I fought back nausea at the sight.

"He's here, now," I told the Mayor gently. "He says that he does love you." The Mayor broke down, then. What do you do when the Mayor of your city is in tears at your kitchen island? I didn't know. His bodyguard and driver were right there, so I didn't think I could just go over there and give him a hug or anything.

I was thinking that maybe he should have brought along a more demonstrative employee when Shane let himself in the back door. He took one look at the crowd in the kitchen and gave me a lifted eyebrow that said we might be about to have words. Thankfully, Doctor Mitchell went to comfort the Mayor.

"What the hell is going on here?" Shane muttered while nodding to the two police officers, the bodyguard and driver. The Mayor now had his head buried against Melford's shoulder and Melford was awkwardly patting the Mayor's back. Yeah, I know. I called him Melford.

Garegar leaned against the refrigerator, taking in the scene before him with a great deal of interest. I stood next to Shane, who waited impatiently for me to tell him why there were six strangers in my house. I ignored him and his accusatory stare. The Mayor had slackened off so Melford handed him a tissue—the man had a packet of them tucked away somewhere. Hey, maybe he'd been a boy scout. You never know.

The Mayor looked up at me, now, wiped his eyes with the tissue and said "Thank you for the information, Mrs. Francis. What you told the detectives here really helped us out. At least we can get the assistance we need for Kristen. I had no idea Libby's brother would have ever," he let the sentence drop. I nodded my head in understanding. He rose from his seat, shook my hand and thanked me for the tea and cookies. He and his entourage left shortly afterward, which meant that Melford and the two officers were still there.

"Uh, Mrs. Francis," one of the officers began, "We were wondering if you wouldn't mind, oh, every once in a while, coming to visit a crime scene or something to oh, you know, help out a little?" He seemed uncomfortable asking the question. I was uncomfortable that he asked.

Shane and I both stiffened. I didn't want to have anything to do with that. Yeah, I might be able to help, but I already had more than enough to take up my time, and what if those poor souls wanted a message delivered in the middle of all that? They found me often enough as it was, either to escort them across or deliver a message for them.

I was already shaking my head; I wasn't about to volunteer for that. No way. That officer, though, he had sad eyes. Big, sad, bloodhound eyes. I sighed. "All right, but only three times a year. You got that? Three trips to a crime scene, and you'd better not let this out to anybody else, you hear me? Otherwise, the deal's off."

"Yes, Mrs. Francis," both men nodded and did their best to get the hell out of my house before I changed my mind. Shane stared at me as if I'd lost my mind (which in all probability, I had). I followed the officers to the door like a good Southern hostess, waved at them as they climbed into their cruiser and backed out of the driveway. Five down, one to go. I squared my shoulders and hobbled back to the kitchen, where Shane and Melford waited. Garegar was still there, as was Sam.

"Conner Louella," Shane had fists on his hips when I came in, and

Melford attempted to make himself smaller; he knew the rant was about to descend. I had no idea why somebody in so much need of therapy himself had chosen a career in psychiatry.

"Shane, just wait a minute," I turned to Melford. "Melford," I said, "If you don't like what you're doing, go do something else. Your mother is long gone, she's not here, darlin'. You get to do what you want from now on."

Melford gaped at me as if I'd lost my mind, and in his profession, that definitely wasn't a compliment. "She's really not here?" He asked after a few minutes.

"Honey, I haven't seen anybody with you since I first laid eyes on you. So if you think there's somebody there, well, there's not. Maybe you ought to go over to Buford and see somebody there, since you probably don't want anybody in Atlanta knowin'."

"I know somebody in Savannah," he said, thinking hard.

"Good enough," I held my hands out in acceptance. Melford slipped off his barstool and actually smiled at me. Shane, Garegar, Sam and I followed him to the front door and watched him climb into his Mercedes. Hey, he might dislike his job, but it apparently paid well. "Now," I said, looking at the small group that was left, "only two more things to do. Come out, mama bear."

I put the *command* into my voice this time, and Melford's mother didn't have a choice but to appear. Some older ghosts can hide their appearance from me, at least for a while. But once I know they're there, they can't disobey me. It was one of the perks of what I could do.

She had her hair swept up in what I imagined was a heavily hair sprayed coif, and the severity of it transferred to her face and stance. "What do you want?" She tried to get her bluff in on me, just as she'd done with her son. She had no idea what I could do. None.

"Oh, no you don't," I told her. "You and I are gonna take a little trip. You're gonna leave that boy alone. He's in his forties, for Pete's sake," I said. "He gets to make his mind up from now on without you nagging in his ear."

Shane knew what was coming, so we ushered Mom Mitchell into

the sitting room nearby where I could lie down and go into my trance. Garegar and Sam followed along behind, curious about what I was going to do. Settling on the sofa, I went into my trance (Shane knows to watch over me because my heartbeat and breathing slow down so much I appear dead when I do this) then allowed my spirit to leave my body. Mom Mitchell was quite surprised when my spirit stood next to hers. I took her by the hand, which she now could feel, and together we found that place that whisked us right to the gate.

The gates are never in the same place twice, or if they are, they look different. Sometimes there are fields of flowers when we arrive. Or an ocean with surf piling up on a sandy beach. I've seen forests, mountains, valleys and rivers. Those are the good ones—the nice gates. The not so good ones, well, the best of those are a rocky barren. This one had outcroppings of jagged black rocks, obsidian-like and sharp as knives. The gate was past that, and I glared an accusation at Mom Mitchell. "Somebody was a bad girl," I informed her.

"I don't want to go in there," she said, backing away.

"But you are going in there," I said. "Go. You should have gone when you had the chance before. I have a feeling that staying behind to torture your child made this worse than it was."

She slashed at me, attempting to claw my face, but her hands passed right through me. "Uh-uh," I told her. "Go now or I'll get forceful, and you don't want that to happen."

That's when she really turned on me, or tried to. That wasn't going to happen. Not to someone like me. I picked her up bodily (I know she was a spirit, but this is harder than it sounds, especially if every fiber of their being is resistant), and threw her like a spear through the open portal. She shrieked when she passed through. The gate closed immediately after, the scream cut off and I dusted off my hands in satisfaction. Then, I straightened my ghostly clothing, got myself back in hand and made the return journey to my waiting body.

"Thank goodness," Shane sighed when I opened my eyes. He always freaks when I do this, although I've never failed to come back. Garegar and Sam were hovering over Shane's shoulder as I blinked up at all of them.

"Yeah," I said. "Nice to see you guys, too." I sat up on the sofa; I always have a terrible headache after these things—apparently those wasted landscapes are a horror unto themselves. The nicer places, though, I don't hurt anywhere when I come back from those.

"Come on, Conner, let's get you something to eat," Shane pulled me off the sofa and helped me hobble toward the kitchen. My foot was throbbing again. I was thinking about asking for ibuprofen when Garegar decided to make his presence known to Shane; he lifted me and carried me the rest of the way to the kitchen. He was kind enough to fix my headache and my foot while Shane gave him wide-eyed glances and made a cheese sandwich for me.

"How long has he been here?" Shane whispered when Garegar stepped away from me for a few moments.

"Since yesterday," I said in my normal voice. "Don't worry, his kind don't mean any harm."

"He's huge," Shane was still whispering. "How the hell do you know he doesn't mean any harm?"

"He drove me home, yesterday," I said. "Even though he doesn't have a license and didn't know how to drive."

"Those are not stellar qualifications, Conner Louella," Shane had his hands on his hips again.

"Maybe not," I agreed, "but he got me home and didn't break the speed limit once. I'm thinkin' he's mighty fine. Maybe I'll adopt him."

Garegar grinned at my statement. I turned to Sam. "Sam, are you ready to go over, or did you want to stay for a while?"

"Is it all right if I stay for a while, to watch over sis?" he asked. "She might need some help."

"Good help is always smiled upon," I told him. "I'll be here, I reckon, when you're ready to go."

"I'll find you," he promised. "Happy New Year," he added and disappeared.

Garegar came to me next, and leaned down to kiss my cheek. "I must go now, also," he said. "It has been a greater pleasure than I can describe." He smiled and disappeared as well.

"Just who the hell was he?" Shane demanded.

"Garegar," I replied with a shrug. "He said he was Larentii."

"Child," Graegar the Wise One said to his son, "When we gave you permission to visit your mother, we had no idea you would choose that portion of her life."

"Father, I wanted to see her before she was brought over—before she became what she is, now. When she became the Guardian, things were made easier. This gave me a glimpse into her life when things were difficult. I learned what a strong person my mother is."

"Yes, your mother has always been that," the Wise One agreed.

"Father, do you think she might have recognized me? She said she wanted to adopt me."

"My son, I cannot say what your mother may or may not know. I have a feeling that she will be demanding to see you for herself before long. We will take you. Bear in mind that the Liaisons have had to go back and wipe the memories from both her mind and Shane's. The journal she kept that held the information was also confiscated and is now placed in the Larentii archives. Yours are the only memories, now, of your visit there."

"That is such a shame, father. It was more entertaining than I can say."

The End

QUEEN'S HOLIDAY

CHAPTER 1

Queen's Palace, Le-Ath Veronis
Lissa
"I think we should go on vacation."

Not only did Breanne startle me when she appeared from nowhere inside my study, but her words shocked the hell out of me.

"Vacation?" My voice was an embarrassing squeak as I struggled to hide my shock.

"Yeah. Girls only, you know? Resting, drinking, swimming, eating, ignoring anything with a penis?"

"Well, that would certainly be different," I drawled. At least I sounded like I was from Oklahoma, now, instead of from Oklahoma with a mouse's range and timbre.

"Just us?" Frankly, she'd never shown any interest. Hell, she barely showed up once every three years.

"Well, maybe a few others—Kiarra, Grace, Devin, Reah, Quin—Zaria?"

"You think Zaria would come?" That could shock me more than Breanne going, I think.

"I think so."

"When?"

"Next week. Don't tell me you can't clear your calendar, or get somebody to cover for you," she held up a hand.

I couldn't argue with that, especially since she could see right through anybody and tell them more than they knew about themselves already, yours truly included.

"Fine. Wonderful. Where are we going, again?"

"I think Marbool. To see the *Book of Kearling.*"

"That should take ten minutes," I pointed out.

"Refer to the resting, drinking, eating comment," she argued.

"Oh. Why there? They only let you see a page or two of the book. There are plenty of nicer beaches with better restaurants, massages, et cetera," I said.

"Humor me," she smiled.

"All right. I owe you one. Or a hundred. We'll go to Marbool, provided you can convince the others to go and they agree on Marbool."

"Pack your bags, blondie, we're going," she sniffed.

"Strawberry-blonde," I corrected, pulling a few strands of hair around to stare at them. Bree could *Change What Was*—I didn't want to wait until later to discover that she'd turned me completely blonde —like during the afternoon Council meeting or something.

"I have to find a babysitter," I added.

"Like Winkler can't take care of his own kids?" Bree's fists now rested on her hips.

"Winkler can take care of the kids," I conceded. "But they'll be eating brownies for breakfast, guaranteed."

"Tell me that brownies will do anything to a werewolf metabolism, or even a half-werewolf metabolism."

"You got me there," I pointed out. My sarcasm didn't fail to raise my sister's eyebrows, either.

Mission accomplished.

"What's the weather on Marbool?"

"Nice, this time of year. Not too hot, not too cold."

"You know there'll be arguments because we're leaving the guys at home, don't you?"

"Look, if you can't handle being away from them for an eight-day, then invite one or two to spend a night. Days are for the girls."

"Sounds better already."

Avii Castle

Quin

"Zaria says you can visit," I held off Justis' latest argument as I packed clothing in a bag. "Just ask Daragar or one of the others to bring you. It's only an eight-day."

Justis looked as if he'd not see me for months instead of eight days. None of the others were quibbling over a short vacation, but Justis worried; I could see it in the furrowed brow and frown lines around his beautiful mouth.

"Will you be treated with the proper respect?" he demanded.

"My love, I think Zaria would separate particles if I were in any danger," I said, addressing his real concern instead of his actual question.

"What about the hotel? Is it safe enough?"

"Justis," I moved toward him, and placed my hands on his shoulders before standing on tiptoe to kiss him. His arms came around me; his fingers stroked my feathers as he deepened the kiss.

"Has royalty stayed there before?" Justis asked once we broke the kiss. Dark eyes peered into mine, asking me silently whether there'd be enough security on the premises, even with Zaria there to protect me.

"Queen Lissa is going," I reminded him. "And Queen Reah. If that isn't enough to satisfy any related question, then I have nothing else to convince you." I shook my head at the King of the Avii.

"All right, but I expect a report now and then." Arms crossed over his chest.

"All you'll hear is we're having fun," I retorted.

A dark eyebrow lifted, but he knew the matter was closed. "Lissa is on her way," I said. "I believe her Larentii are transporting us to Marbool, so there'll be no problems. I promise."

I was kissing Justis again when Dena tapped on the door, telling us Lissa, Connegar and Reemagar had arrived.

~

Marbool Monarch Hotel and Resort
Kiarra

"This is nice," Grace, Devin and I walked through the hotel lobby on our way to check in. Once we had key codes to our suites, we'd *Pull* our luggage in; there was no need to drag it around with us.

"Lissa, Reah and Quin are already here," Devin's smile showed a dimple as she whispered and pointed at those three standing at the front desk.

"I can't wait to get a drink and sit by the pool," Grace sighed. "Why didn't we think about this before?"

"Because it's harder than digging through granite with a spork to get the guys to let us out of their sight," Devin teased. "If Breanne hadn't put this together, we could still be arguing with all of them, too."

"You know, I think there are maybe ten people in both alliances who actually know what a spork is," Kiarra laughed. "More than half of them are on this trip."

"Less than that call it a foon," Grace giggled.

"Foon? Are you kidding? Somebody really called it that?" Devin asked.

"At least four people."

"It almost sounds dirty," I said. "Wanna go to bed and foon?"

"When you put it like that, it is dirty," Devin snickered.

"I heard the entire conversation from the front desk," Lissa said. She, Reah and Quin joined us at the center of the marble-tiled floor. "Foon? Really? I need a drink."

~

Breanne

Zaria and I didn't have to ask what they were all laughing about when we arrived in the lobby; the others were there and giggling about sporks and fooning.

"I am not telling Phrinnis Tampirus about those things," Zaria joined the conversation and they erupted in fresh giggles.

Phrinnis Tampirus, or Tamp, was one of Zaria's mates and a pod'l-morph. He could become anything animal, vegetable or mineral, although it might be a let-down to see him as a spork—or a foon. Usually he was quite handsome. Converting to a piece of archaic, plastic cutlery certainly wouldn't do him justice.

"I have room codes," Lissa said when the laughter died down. "Are we drinking and carrying on in somebody's suite or at the pool bar?"

"Pool bar," Grace raised a hand.

"Last one out pays," Lissa said and almost ran for the trans-vator.

Zaria

I didn't mind paying, and I'd taken my time getting downstairs to the bar. It was nice to see Quin letting loose—she'd flown from her balcony suite down to the pool area, so she wouldn't be last. Everybody, including the bartenders, were laughing and smiling as they treated her like the royalty she was.

She'd never had a childhood—she'd been put to work from the time she could stand at a sink and wash dishes.

Being an orphan in Fyris was never easy, and Quin's story was harder than most. *That's why I adopted her as my own*, I reminded myself.

"Come on, you're missing all the fun," Breanne pulled me toward the others, who sat around a long table, drinks in front of them while they laughed and talked.

Lissa

I had no idea we'd be forced to take a tour of the grounds and buildings surrounding the library where the *Book of Kearling* was displayed. This was our second-day plan—see the book and get that part out of the way. Going to a remote beach was item three and scheduled for the following day.

"The only gardens which rival these are the gardens surrounding Reth Alliance Founder Ildevar Wyyld's palace," our tour guide spoke as she walked us through an outer corner of the gardens. All sorts of flowers were in bloom, and shrubs and topiaries were carved into strange and wondrous shapes.

"I have heard," our guide, a middle-aged woman, went on, "that the gardens inside Avii Castle's glass walls are beautiful, too, but word has it that tourists aren't allowed inside unless they have permission from the King."

"I've seen them," I raised my hand. "If you ask the Queen, you might get in, too."

"Avii Castle is one of the things I want to do in my life," the woman sounded rapturous. "If you have a name of a secretary or something, so I can get a message to the Queen, I'd appreciate it very much."

"I'll get something to you," I promised.

Quin, who stood nearby, snickered. Zaria had concealed Quin's wings in an invisible shield, so people wouldn't stare and ask questions—we were regular tourists today.

After an hour of walking around Marbool's grounds and other buildings, we were led toward the library, where the *Book of Kearling* waited.

I thought we were getting a private tour, Kiarra sent when we walked into the small room that housed the *Book of Kearling* and nothing else.

Two women—identical twins, stood in a corner, tapping away on comp-vids. Dark skin was complimented by honey-gold eyes, and both wore long, colorful skirts—one in blues and greens, the other in yellows and golds.

The book lay on a pedestal, enveloped in an impenetrable, clear case. They didn't even want anyone to breathe near the book. As advertised, the book was open, showing two pages only, and those weren't the ones we were interested in.

"This is Nari and Tiri, scholars who are doing research on the *Book of Kearling*," our guide introduced the two women in the room. "They know more about the myths and fables surrounding the book than I do. They'll be answering your questions, today."

"I'm interested in the tale that the book contains a dangerous spell at the end," Breanne spoke right away.

"That has never been proven, and the language never deciphered," one of the women spoke. "I am Nari," she introduced herself. "My sister and I have worked for years, trying to translate that portion of the book."

"Are there copies of it?" Quin asked. If anyone could read it, Quin could.

"Copies are as closely guarded as the actual book," Tiri explained. "We've signed contracts to keep that information for our studies only."

"Contracts with whom?" Reah asked.

"The Marboolian Government, of course. Since they have no idea what the book contains, they are understandably reluctant to release that information to anyone." That, I understood clearly, meant that they didn't want to give away their best tourist attraction, when the translation could be somebody's ancient cookie recipe.

"Have other scholars received copies?" Grace asked.

"Only a few are interested. There are many reports from other scholars in the past, all of which say that the language is like nothing they've ever seen."

"What's your opinion, since you've seen it?" Zaria's question came next.

"There are no markers—no correlations," Tiri confessed. "We're still going through the most obscure languages we've ever encountered, and so far, we've found nothing that compares to this one."

"Tell us the legends, then," Devin begged. "I love things like that."

Nari smiled at Devin, the smile lighting her face. She loved things like that, too. "One legend says that portion of the book contains the

35

darkest of spells, which, if spoken, will release demons upon the worlds. Another says it is the spell of rebirth, and will remake the worlds if they are destroyed."

"Those two are the best-known stories," Tiri said.

"What if both are correct?" Zaria asked.

"I don't see how," Nari frowned at Zaria's words.

"It was just a thought," Zaria waved away Nari's concern. "So—you've not encountered a myth, then, that both could be true?"

"Neither of us have," Tiri admitted. "Perhaps that's something to consider."

"What are some of the other myths?" Kiarra asked.

"There's one—although I think they were being sarcastic, that says it was actually a recipe list for drinks," Nari grinned.

"Fake news," Grace and Devin said at the same moment, then laughed and hugged.

"Ah, it's time for the next group," our tour guide cleared her throat.

"Thank you for coming—you've given us something to think about," Nari said. "That doesn't happen, normally."

"If you want, we'll buy your dinner tonight at the Marbool Monarch Hotel," Zaria offered. "We're here on holiday, and there's always room for more ladies at the table."

"That sounds nice," Nari turned toward her sister, silently asking for agreement.

"Just tell the hotel staff you were invited by Lissa," I said. "They'll know to bring you to our table. Around nine bells?"

"Sounds good," Tiri agreed. "We'll see you there."

We were ushered out of the room and straight into a gift shop, cluttered with items to sell, including necklaces and bracelets bearing charms that resembled the closed *Book of Kearling*.

"Who can I give this to?" our tour guide waved a hand-written note.

"I'll take it," Quin said. "It will be presented to the proper person, I promise."

"Have you all seen Avii Castle?" the tour guide sounded breathless.

"Quin lives there," Zaria said, releasing the shield around Quin's wings.

~

Quin

I ended up having to touch the tour guide, whose name was Aderis, to relieve her hyperventilation.

"I can't believe the Avii Queen is here," she kept repeating, until Lissa placed compulsion for her to calm down, and then placed compulsion for her not to remember the compulsion.

"That took longer than I thought," Zaria put an arm around my shoulders as we walked into the hotel later. "What would you like to do now, daughter of my heart?"

"I'd say go flying, but that's tomorrow," I said. "Grace and Devin want to come with us."

Grace was the Lace-Feathered Eagle, and Devin the Driskilhin Night Hawk when they turned—both large raptors, who were more than adept at flying. I was looking forward to exploring Marbool's skies with both.

"It'll be a lesson for me," Zaria sighed. She had wings when she wanted them, but she seldom used them to fly. She always said that folding space was a faster mode of travel. She'd never used her wings for the sheer pleasure of it.

~

Zaria

"We're thinking about doing the dinner cruise tomorrow night," Lissa joined us on our way to the trans-vator. "Here's the information." She handed a comp-vid to Quin.

"Do you think we'll see whales?" Quin turned to blink at Lissa.

"Who knows," she shrugged. "It's worth a try, and the food is supposed to be good. Reah wants to check that out; the chef is supposed to be really good."

"They have space available for all of us?" I asked. "Tomorrow night is short notice."

"They do. Some tourists have canceled and left Marbool. There's a psychic's convention going on at a hotel complex not far away, and half the psychics are predicting doom and gloom, for some reason."

"Really? Why would they do that?" Quin asked.

"No idea," Lissa replied. "I just overheard some employees talking about it. They didn't think I could hear them."

Lissa was vampire, so of course she'd hear them, whereas a normal person wouldn't.

"What was their take on the doom and gloom?" I asked.

"They were worried that it would affect their seasonal tips," Lissa shrugged.

"Which hotel?" I asked.

"The Groves, about a mile east," she said.

"Hmmm."

"You're thinking about checking it out?"

"I may."

"I was thinking about sitting by the pool with some fruit and cheese," Lissa said.

"May I join you?" Quin asked.

"Absolutely. We'll let Zaria do her sleuthing, and the rest of us will relax and talk. Don't forget dinner at nine with Nari and Tiri," Lissa reminded me.

"I won't," I promised and headed for the exit.

The Groves wasn't as highly-rated as the Marbool Monarch, but it was the one that hosted conventions more often than not. The moment I walked into the lobby, I found it filled with those who had actual psychic ability, some who claimed to be psychics and those who could only wish to be.

I suppose those wishing to be psychics hoped that talent would rub off on them if they knocked elbows with the others.

According to an electronic message board in the lobby, the public would be allowed to meet with psychics the following day, to have their palms read, their cards read, or any number of other things.

"I had no idea the Brothers of the Dark Moon would show up," someone said to their companions as they walked past me. "They didn't make reservations or send in registration forms."

"Where are they staying?" Someone else asked. "This hotel is full— or was, until some of us left." Her last words were coated with sarcasm.

"The Gardens, I think," the original speaker replied, naming another hotel a block away. "I think they're trying to cut into our event, without putting out the money. They'll draw some of our crowd away, just watch."

The Brothers of the Dark Moon—they were the ones famous for predicting the end of the Alliances, end of planets, end of universes, ad nauseam.

There was no other choice; I'd have to visit the Gardens Hotel, too.

I'd come back to this hotel the following day, just to listen to what the psychics here were saying—those who'd chosen to stay, anyway. I'd read in several that some of their big names had decided to leave early, with no clear excuse given, other than they felt bad vibes or something.

The others, well, either they were adept at ignoring things, or their ability wasn't as strong as they'd like it to be.

Time to visit the Brothers, and see what they were up to.

CHAPTER 2

Z aria

The Gardens Hotel was owned by the same conglomerate that owned the Groves Hotel, and looked similar in style and taste. Only a few Brothers were out and about, however, their long, gray robes dusting marble floors as they walked here or there.

"Do you suppose they really know anything?" Breanne appeared at my side.

"If they do, they haven't passed the messages to these guys," I tilted my head toward three robe-clad Brothers walking toward the front desk.

"You think the big-wigs are waiting to say something—intentionally? So the lesser members won't take off running?"

"Maybe, and it worries me. They're all men, you know."

"And that worries *me*," Breanne agreed. "Usually, they're harmless, and get together to drink and carouse before coming up with their crackpot doomsday reports."

"Yeah. They always make the news-vids, though, so we may have journalists to deal with, too."

"Then I say we go find some of those," Bree suggested.

"The bars here should be a good place to start," I said.
"Let's go."

Marbool Monarch Hotel
Lissa

"I got mindspeech from Bree—they're at a bar at the Gardens Hotel," I said. "The psychics at the Groves were boring, apparently, so they went to watch the Brothers of the Dark Moon, who are hanging out at the Gardens."

"Those guys?" Kiarra snickered. "I heard they were a hedonistic bunch masquerading as a legitimate prophetic religion—and I do use that term loosely."

We sat at a table in the pool bar, while bartenders and servers argued over who'd bring us the next round of drinks. They all wanted to gawk at Quin's wings, and once word got out that High Demon Queen Reah was with us, too, they all wanted to wait on us.

So far, they hadn't figured out that the Vampire Queen of Le-Ath Veronis was here as well, and that suited me fine.

After all, if they bothered Quin and Reah too much, there was always friendly compulsion. *When are you two coming back?* I sent to Bree.

Give us some time—actually, we can bend time, she replied. *We'll be back in time for dinner, don't worry.*

Fine, I returned. *Just let me know if you need me to send out the dogs.*

Why would we need that?

Come on, I know you're not telling me something, I pointed out. *I think the others know, too, they're just going along, pretending not to know.*

Fine. Look, we'll have a meeting in a day or two, and we can tell you what little we know then.

Good. I hate when something is going on and nobody tells me anything.

I know that about you, my sister responded.

I figure you do, I said dryly.

Oh—gotta go—we just found a journalist and he's half drunk. Score, she said and cut off her mindspeech.

A journalist? What the hell did she want one of those for? "I'd like another," I held up my empty drink glass to let our attentive server know while I pondered that question.

$$\sim$$

The Gardens Hotel
Zaria

"Well, well, ladies, what can I get for you," he smiled at us. Barlok Mewws, field reporter for News Nine-Ninety-Nine, grinned and motioned for us to sit beside him at the bar.

"Why Barlok Mewws," Breanne grinned. "What brings you to Marbool?"

"Just following the Brothers of the Dark Moon," he laughed.

"Have you interviewed any of them?" Breanne asked.

"Have an interview set up with the Master of the Dark Moon tomorrow morning," he said. "Come on, let me buy you a drink."

"Why don't you let us buy you one?" I asked.

"That works," he said. "It's boring, talking to those guys—I've done research on their crazy predictions already, and I don't need to hear—again—that they predicted the fall of the banking system on Veemera."

"Any economist could have predicted that," Bree snorted. "In fact, several did."

"I like you," Barlok leered at Bree.

"Lots of people do," she agreed.

"Need help?" Trajan, Bree's seven-foot werewolf mate, stepped in beside Breanne.

"Who are you?" Barlok lifted an eyebrow and sounded haughty at the same time. Sure, Barlok could multitask, but it didn't matter if he knew every martial art in the universes; Trajan would still wipe the floor with him.

"Honey, I'm fine," Bree smiled up at Trajan. Trajan's appearance made Barlok turn his attention immediately to me, and that wasn't a good thing.

"Ilya Ironsmith," Ilya stuck his hand in-between Barlok and me, grabbing Barlok's hand before he had a chance to touch me.

"Uh, Barlok Mewws," Barlok whispered, attempting to pull his crushed hand away from Ilya's grip.

"You did not win at arm wrestling—I still have two hands left," Bleek appeared, with all four arms crossed over his chest as he glared at Ilya. Ilya let Barlok's hand drop as he turned toward Bleek.

"You were arm wrestling to see who'd come?" I frowned at both.

"Is that a—Blevakian?" Barlok was in the process of massaging feeling into his crushed hand while staring at Bleek.

"Step aside, warlock, I have this," Bleek attempted to shove Ilya out of the way.

"Ahem."

Oh, lord.

"Charles?" Breanne turned toward him. Sure—he was one of her mates.

He was also my father—and he'd decided to show up *now*.

"Backing away now," Ilya held up his hands and stepped out of Charles' way.

"Come on, behemoth, she has another side, you know," Ilya pulled Bleek to my other side. Barlok, unsure why the other males, all of whom looked infinitely more dangerous, were moving out of Charles' way, blinked as Charles moved in between Barlok and me. I gave him my chair and moved one down, forcing Ilya and Bleek to do the same.

"Thanks, baby," he winked at me before turning to Barlok.

"Who are you?" Barlok demanded rudely.

"Her father," he nodded toward me, "and her husband—one of them," he nodded toward Bree. "Now, hand it over." Charles held out a hand.

Barlok's eyes went strange as he fished in his pocket before pulling something small out and placing it in Charles' hands.

Yeah, Bree and I both knew he had it. I'd already rendered it useless, but Charles wanted to go one further, I suppose.

Trajan's growl almost made Barlok wet his pants.

"Geeni," Charles sighed, pronouncing the word like genie, as he held up the small packet of drugs. "I'd like to know where you got this —for future reference, you understand."

"You uh, want some?" Barlok quavered.

"I already have this, and the ASD is on the way," Charles shrugged, waving the small packet in front of Barlok's face. Barlok cringed and shrank back on his seat.

"Kooper, he's all yours," Charles handed the packet to Kooper, who'd arrived in record time. "I think Barlok will have some interesting information to tell you—won't you, Barlok?" Charles turned back toward the journalist, whose eyes had gone strange.

Charles was placing compulsion, as only the Mighty Mind might do it.

The rest of us watched as Kooper and two agents pulled Barlok out of the bar in wrist cuffs.

"We wanted to sit in on his interview with the Master of the Dark Moon," Breanne told Charles. "Now, that's all messed up."

"No, sweetheart," he soothed. "We have plenty of people, any one of whom can take Barlok's place tomorrow morning."

"Who?" Breanne's arms crossed over her chest, making me think of Bleek for a moment.

"I'd suggest either Rigo, Merrill or—me."

"Are you telling me that this may be the worst-kept secret of all-time?"

"It's not nearly that bad," Charles began.

"Oh, for cripes' sake," I blew out a sigh.

"Sure. Try to keep the testosterone out of this, because goodness knows they could be in danger, and what happens?" Breanne tossed up a hand in resignation.

"Look, we'll be out of here in plenty of time," Trajan said.

"Not you, too," Breanne covered her face with both hands.

"Ashe said it was a good idea," Trajan defended himself.

"Right. Has he been to the Larentii Archives to read their copy of the book, too?" I asked as sweetly as I could.

"He didn't say."

"Did he know that only birds and certain other creatures can read

44

all of the book's words?" Breanne asked. "Because some of them are in colors that humans and most humanoids can't see."

"Are you telling me that a chicken can read the book, and I can't?" Trajan asked.

"That's what I'm saying, yes," Breanne huffed.

"How did you get that information, then?" Trajan demanded. Charles smiled but refused to comment.

"You've never seen Nefrigar as a chicken? I'm shocked," Breanne teased.

She'd named my Larentii father-in-law, who was Chief Archivist in the Larentii Archives. "Actually, he read it as a Baridian Mountain Cat," I explained before Trajan started making fun of chickens. "They can see the proper color spectrum, too."

"So, what did it say?" Ilya asked.

"It's cryptic, but we've sorted it out far enough to understand that whatever may be hiding in the book will choose his next weapon to inflict doom upon the worlds."

"Then how do you know it'll be male?" Trajan queried.

"Because there's an image of a naked humanoid, and there's little doubt that it's male," Breanne sniffed.

"So, there's something hiding in the book, waiting to take somebody—a male somebody—over, to create havoc?"

"That's what we've determined so far—plus the fact that it also intends to take an army of males to help him do his dirty work—also depicted in images no humanoid can see."

"And that's why you're worried about the Brothers," Bleek sighed. "An all-male group who'd raise their hands to be chosen first."

"Yep," I said. "They'll be all over that, if they find out about it."

"Have you felt this—presence—in the book? When you went to see it?" Charles asked.

"I could feel it half a light-year away from here," Breanne frowned at Charles. "It's making its presence known after lying dormant since the book was written."

"That's nearly two-thousand years, according to Ashe," Trajan said.

"Is there anything else written about this—entity?" Ilya asked.

"Nefrigar hasn't found anything," I said. "And he and his sons have searched for nearly as long as the book has existed."

"Who wrote the book?" Bleek asked.

"A monk in a religious order—but he didn't write the last part—the one we're concerned with," Breanne lifted her shoulders in a shrug. "Zaria and I went back to check on that. The monk died before he filled in the last few pages. The book sat in the religious order's library for a few years, and when it was opened again, it had the added section at the back. No evidence that the book was moved at any time while it sat on that shelf."

"So that's why the first part can be deciphered, and the last part can't," Trajan looked thoughtful.

"And the scholars who've studied the book assume it was all written by the same person, because the monk was suffering from dementia there at the last. Just looking at the text at the back without knowing it has colors added outside your normal spectrum—you'd assume it was the same person writing it, but writing in gibberish. Who or whatever wrote that part even made the ink the same—what you can see of it, anyway."

"That's an easy spell," Ilya pointed out. "A first-level warlock or witch could do that."

"Yes, but hiding your identity—even from the Larentii—that's much more complicated," Charles observed.

"True," Ilya conceded.

"I'm thinking about going back," Breanne said. "Bending time so I can see the book on the shelf where it lay for six years before somebody thought to open it."

"I may go back a little further," I said. "I want to watch the monk writing his last page. I may meet you in the library later," I told Breanne.

"Sounds good. Don't tire yourself—we still have to make dinner tonight," she cautioned.

"I'll remember. Well, honey," I kissed Ilya, "Honey," I kissed Bleek, "See ya." I bent time and folded space.

CHAPTER 3

*P*ast—*Marbool*
      Zaria

The monastery, towering over the other structures in Marbool's early days, was built of wood and rough-hewn rock. A nearby lake provided water for the monks and for the small town surrounding the monastery. It was late summer; no rain had fallen for weeks and the lake smelled stagnant from my place just outside the walls.

The unsanitary possibilities made me want to shiver in Marbool's summer heat, as the stench of outdoor trenches and outhouses wafted past with the occasional, lazy breeze. *Time to go inside and visit the monk*, I reminded myself. The following day, he'd fall ill and wouldn't rise from his bed again.

I'd already shielded myself from prying eyes—and from anyone with sufficient power to search for my presence. If the entity were already present, I had no desire to let him know.

Folding space brought me into the monk's quarters, where he sat at a table, bent over his work. By now, his meticulous script had begun to wander through the letters and words he wrote—dementia was taking its toll.

The other monks knew of his condition, but as the book kept him occupied, they'd let him proceed undisturbed.

Probably why they left it on the shelf for so long after his death—they knew the last part he'd written was mostly gibberish.

He hadn't swept his quarters in a while, either; mouse droppings lay here and there, and the occasional cockroach was brave enough to scuttle from the wall toward dropped crumbs of bread beneath the table.

I had no idea why the other monks hadn't attempted to tidy up, but they obviously had a mouse and bug problem throughout, unless I missed my guess. The monk's unemptied chamber pot only added to my already rising gag factor.

I left in a hurry; bending time to join Bree in the library.

"Nothing," Bree shook her head at me when I arrived three years later in the library. "Bugs and mice all over—half the books are nibbled on by the mice, as you may expect."

"I saw the same thing in the monk's quarters," I agreed. "The smell of the place, too—man it was awful."

"At least they keep the library floor as clean as they can under the circumstances. It's swept every day, to remove evidence of the vermin."

"It isn't so dry this time," I said. "They were having a drought the summer the monk died."

"Find anything else?" Bree asked.

"Nothing. Absolutely-fucking-nothing."

"Same here. Waste of time," she sighed. "Well, let's go back. We have time for a drink before we go to dinner."

"I'm with you," I said. Bree bent time and folded space, taking me with her.

Marbool Monarch Hotel

Lissa

"Find anything?" I asked when Bree and Zaria joined me at my pool-side table.

"Not a damn thing," Bree shook her head. "Just primitive living conditions, ugly smells, bugs and mice."

"What can I get for you ladies?" An attentive waiter appeared at our table.

"I want a French martini," Zaria said. "Wait, you don't know what that is, do you?"

"I've never heard of it," he shook his head.

"She wants a Viltem squeeze with raspberry liqueur," Bree said. "I'll have one, too."

"Right away," the waiter smiled and trotted toward the bar.

"Three of those and you're drunk," I pointed out.

"I was hoping to get drunk," Zaria nodded. "Please don't destroy my dreams and aspirations."

"I think we're trying to get the stench of open trenches and festering outhouses out of our noses," Bree pointed out. "Leave us some hope, okay?"

"When you put it like that," I said and lifted my own drink in a toast.

Nari

"They make my senses tingle; that's all I know," Tiri said as we were dropped off by hover-cab at the Monarch Hotel. We were discussing the eight women who'd come to see the book and spent time discussing it with us earlier.

"They *really* make my senses tingle," I confessed as we walked toward the front entrance. "When they invited us to dinner, it was almost too good to be true. I haven't felt this excited since I saw the *Book of Kearling* the first time."

"Except this is a good tingle, not a bad one," Tiri pointed out.

"True. I'm hoping they can help us sort through this. The tingling is getting worse. I overheard several tourists talking about how some of the best-known psychics have left the convention, because things didn't feel right."

"We both know the Brothers of the Dark Moon are camped out at the Gardens Hotel," Tiri sighed. "They could be onto something real, this time."

"Grandmother Diri would be so proud to know that we inherited her gifts," I said, allowing my shoulders to sag. She'd died far too soon —some said she was killed, but we'd never uncovered proof of it. Our gifts hadn't manifested before she died, either, so she hadn't known that the talent didn't stop with our mother.

Grandmother had spent most of her life tracking dangerous artifacts and rendering them harmless—all anonymously.

Tiri and I worried that something or someone had learned of her mission, and taken steps to eliminate her.

That's why Tiri and I were masters in several fighting arts—we practiced every day, early, so no one else would know. It never hurt to know how to protect yourself.

Our next goal, once we sorted out the *Book of Kearling*, was to travel to Falchan and train with a blademaster there. Lessons could be had, if a blademaster chose to take a student. We were determined to be chosen.

"We're here to have dinner with Lissa's party," Tiri told the host stationed outside the Monarch's best restaurant.

"Of course. Right this way," he smiled and led us into the restaurant.

Lissa

"It's so nice to see you again," Devin greeted our guests as they were seated between her and Grace. Both women glowed from the inside out, their mahogany skin flawless, their dresses, turquoise blue and pale yellow, complimenting everything about them.

"We have a confession to make," Nari began after the host left us.

"Yes. We ah, felt a tingling when you walked into the display room," Tiri took up the conversation.

"As did we," Kiarra smiled back at the twins. "That's why we invited you to dinner."

"It's why we accepted," Nari laughed.

"Good. Now, for proper introductions," I said. "This is Quin, Queen of the Avii," I nodded to Quin. "Kiarra of the Saa Thalarr, Grace of the Saa Thalarr, Devin of the Saa Thalarr, Reah, Queen of the High Demon Planet Kifirin, Breanne, Zaria, and I'm Lissa, Queen of Le-Ath Veronis."

Both women had covered their mouths with their hands, to hide the O of surprise, I figured.

"You don't have titles?" Nari regained her composure first, and pointed her question toward Zaria and Bree.

"We do, but they fall into the *I'm not sure that's real* category," Breanne grinned. "Just call us Zaria and Bree. It's easier, trust me."

"I suppose you'd like to ask us questions about the *Book of Kearling?*" Tiri lifted a delicate eyebrow.

"We may be able to give you some information, too," Bree said. "After dinner, of course. I'm starved. Let's order."

Queen's Palace, Le-Ath Veronis

Quin

"How did we get here?" Nari asked as she and Tiri studied Lissa's library.

"It's called folding space," Lissa said. "It's the best place I know to meet with Connegar and Reemagar. They'll take us to our next destination."

"Ah, good, you have the relic wardens with you," Connegar said as he and Reemagar appeared in Lissa's library. "We are most pleased to meet you," he dipped his head to Nari and Tiri.

~

Nari

Larentii? Tiri's voice sounded in my head. *I never thought we'd see any.*

As twins, we'd always had this method of communication between us. It was more than useful. "Where are we going from here?" I tried to keep the breathless anticipation from my voice.

Larentii.

Larentii Archives. Oh, please say that, I begged mentally.

"You are correct," the one called Connegar smiled, the white of his teeth illuminating the blue of his skin. "We are taking you to Nefrigar, the Chief Archivist, and he will tell you what he knows about the *Book of Kearling*."

He'd either heard me, or he'd pulled the thoughts from my mind. As a Larentii, he could probably do either.

He called us Relic Wardens, Tiri turned to grin at me. *I like that.* It was all she had time to say. The Larentii moved us to another place—possibly the most wondrous place—we'd ever been.

~

Larentii Archives

Lissa

"Hello, dearest," Nefrigar lifted Reah in his arms and held her while they exchanged a kiss.

Tiri turned to give me a look that said *did you see that? I sure did.*

I squelched a snicker in reply.

~

"I've designed filters, so that anyone can see the hidden images and colors represented in Kearling's Book," Nefrigar set the square, monitor-like gadget in front of his copy of the book. "The book isn't named after the monk who wrote it," he added, "but after his former monastery. That monastery was destroyed in a fire, forcing him and his fellow survivors to find other monasteries to take them in."

Tiri and Nari looked at one another, exchanging twin-speak. They hadn't known that, and the Kearling monastery wasn't listed in any of their records.

It wasn't a surprise, since nothing survived of that monastery except a handful of monks. Every book, manuscript and other evidence of its existence was destroyed in the fire.

Nefrigar set the filters to the proper setting, bringing the hidden images in the book to the fore. Tiri and Nari gasped at the same moment, stunned by what they saw.

"This looks like someone is planning a coup," Nari looked up at Nefrigar. "Someone with power."

"We suspect as much, too," Nefrigar agreed. "But we cannot delve past the power in the images to learn who or why. Every time the attempt is made, it's as if the maker and his purpose flees, leaving us with empty blots of hidden ink on a page."

"That's terrifying," Tiri breathed as she leaned in to examine the images closely. "I've never imagined that the book contained anything like this."

"This opens up so many possibilities," Nari agreed. "We'd have to study this carefully to determine what it means."

"You must study quickly," Nefrigar warned. "In our reckoning, the date of this coup is swiftly approaching.'

"How soon?" Nari asked.

"In six days," Nefrigar replied.

"Are you saying you've read the unusual script? Even with the added colors and such, we've still not seen that language before," Nari said.

"I read it—with assistance from my dear friend Quin."

I turned toward Quin, who blushed. She'd known, too, even before we left Le-Ath Veronis, that something was up with the book. It was evident that Nefrigar, Zaria and Breanne had held extended conversations about it as well.

"Quin can read or decipher anything, and, as an Avii, she has the proper eyesight to see all the hidden colors and images without the aid of filters," Nefrigar sounded proud.

"I can provide copies of all the images, but as I've said, we have limited time," the Chief Archivist warned the scholars. "I think it will be up to you and the others here, to sort this out. I feel this book is extremely dangerous to any normal male who is close to it when the time comes."

"So those with power may be immune?" Kiarra asked.

"Perhaps. They may have to be very powerful to avoid the effects, which, according to the images, look to be quite devastating."

"I never thought we'd figure out this book," Nari shook her head while peering closely at the images. "Now that we've seen its secrets— in a way, at least—a part of me wishes we hadn't."

"That's the way things usually go," Grace soothed. "But I think we've been brought together for a reason, so take comfort in that, if nothing else."

"Six days." Tiri shook her head this time. "Nari, we have work to do," she said.

Marbool Monarch Hotel
  Zaria
  We rented an extra suite on our floor for the twins, so they could stay in comfort while we worked on the conundrum presented by the *Book of Kearling*.

I sat in a corner of their suite, drinking tea and listening while Quin read passages for them from the hidden section.

Quin trusted both; she'd let her wings droop and draggle, relaxing them while they worked on the page copies Nefrigar provided.

I committed the images to my memory—Quin, beautiful in the morning light, her red wings falling away behind her like a magnificent, scarlet train of feathers. Nari and Tiri, the sun making their skin glisten, their dark hair pulled back and tied in intricate, lovely knots, their eyes shining as they paid rapt attention to Quin's readings. Occasionally they spoke mentally, attempting to sort out the riddles in the words.

Our flying excursion had been postponed—I hoped Quin would have the opportunity to fly with Grace and Devin when this was over; I was willing to let them fly wherever they wanted if we sorted out this apocalypse before it happened, and found a way to stop it.

Bree, Kiarra and Lissa had gone to the Gardens Hotel, to be there when Charles did his interview with the Master of the Dark Moon. I was waiting to hear what he had to say on the subject, or whether he knew anything at all.

Grace and Devin had gone back to the building which housed the *Book of Kearling*, strolling the gardens outside and watching for anyone or anything unusual to approach. They sent regular reports in mindspeech, but so far, they'd only reported a child who'd vomited on a rosebush, prompting the appearance of a robotic med-unit.

Bree, your vacations suck, I sent to her.

Lissa already told me that—twice.

Want me to say it again?

No.

How's the interview coming along?

They're still in there. Charles must be grilling him on both sides, and poking him with a fork to see if he's cooked long enough.

Interesting barbecue reference, I replied. *Well done.*

I'm laughing on the inside, she returned.

Lissa

"He doesn't know anything," Charles sounded annoyed after casting off the disguise he'd concocted, making him look like the journalist Barlok Mewws. "He found out about the psychic convention. And, since the psychic organizations tend to call his Brotherhood—and I use that term loosely—a mountain of convoluted cow shit, he decided to show up and give them grief. Now that he's here and some of the best psychics have left because they're worried something's about to happen, the Brothers have settled in with a tub of popcorn to watch the circus."

"Can't we tell them to just go home?" Kiarra frowned at Charles.

"I say let them stay. They may have a useful role to play before it's over," Charles said, his words sounding cryptic.

So. There it was. One didn't argue with Wisdom, a.k.a. the Mighty Mind, although one wanted to, from time to time.

Charles lifted an eyebrow at Kiarra. Her frown deepened.

I understood something at that moment—something Breanne and Zaria likely knew already.

Charles was Kiarra's father. And, unless I missed my guess, they were having a friendly argument in mindspeech.

Does this mean? I sent to Zaria.

We're half-sisters, Kiarra, Conner and I, she gave a mental sigh with her answer. *We're still trying to work through this,* she added. *Mostly because I don't call him Dad or Pop or any other form of the term Father. Conner and I never saw him while we were growing up. Kee saw him several times, although he suppressed those memories after. We still haven't discussed all that.*

I understand not being completely on board with the Dad thing, I agreed.

Yeah. You still hold the trophy for worst dad, though. Not that it's a good thing, she added.

Yeah.

CHAPTER 4

*Q*uin

  The last four days passed in a blur, with no new developments. Nari, Tiri and I found no new meanings in any of the words at the back of the book. It appeared to be straightforward, written in what looked to be the *royal we*, and never naming the one intending to bring doom with his gathered troops— all men, of course.

  The drawn images showed the same; men who were taken by the one who'd written those pages. Men, fighting and killing an undepicted foe, to gain control of the worlds. I think my wings drooped a little more as each day passed, when we got no further and gained no new insights.

  We now had roughly a day to avert disaster, and no ideas on how to accomplish that. Until Nari looked up from the page she studied and blinked.

  "Was Zaria serious when she said she went back to the monastery where the book was?" She turned toward me, dark eyes begging me to say yes.

  "She can bend time," I acknowledged. I didn't say that she'd taken me with her a time or two.

"Did anyone look at the books beside this one—in the monks' library?"

I held my breath for a moment as the possibilities hit me. "I don't think so. Nefrigar may have copies," I began.

"I think we should look at the originals," Tiri was immediately on board with her sister. "It may make some minute difference— something that we can use to sort this out. We've never touched the *Book of Kearling*, either. Perhaps it's time we did."

"Let me get Zaria," I folded my wings into their normal, walking position. "We'll ask if she thinks it wise to revisit the past."

"I don't know that any of the other books survived," Zaria had listened carefully as we presented our thoughts to her a few minutes later. "Nari may be right—we've only looked at copies so far. Maybe it is time to look at originals; here and in the past."

"What's this about going on an excursion?" Lissa and Breanne folded into the suite to join us. Both were dressed as if going for a long walk, in jeans and comfortable shoes.

"We're going back to the monastery," Zaria made up her mind. "To look at the *Book of Kearling*, as well as the books on the shelf beside it."

"Do you think they may hold clues—the other books?" Lissa wore a hopeful expression.

"It's worth a try," Tiri said. "We've got nothing here, and we've been through these pages so many times we've memorized them."

"Are we ready to go, then?" Breanne asked. "Kee and the others will be watching the book here while we're gone."

"We're ready," Nari said.

"Me, too," Quin agreed.

"Then let's go." Breanne was the one to bend time, taking us with her.

Zaria

"The monks are at daily meditation, so we have roughly an hour," Bree told us as she set us down in the monastery's library. "Here's the *Book of Kearling*," she pointed to a shelf behind her. "Grab a book near it and start looking. We may have to hurry."

"Oh, gross—cockroach poop," Lissa complained as she opened the book she'd selected. "Looks like the bugs developed a liking for books —they've eaten into the pages," she added, holding the book by a corner as if she found it disgusting.

Frankly, I felt the same, so I placed shields around my hands and pulled a book off the shelf to look. Cockroach spoor and mouse droppings covered the top of the book I'd selected. Determined to keep all of it intact, I employed power to hold those things in place while I studied the book's contents.

Tiri, Nari and Quin had the foresight to bring cotton gloves, and pulled those on before taking books off the shelf.

"You're not going to believe this," I said after reading the archaic language in my book for a moment.

"What's that?" Bree looked up from her book.

"This book is about keeping yourself clean and holy—by avoiding the temptation of soiling yourself with women," I replied.

"That's true," Nari looked up from the volume she held. "While many religious orders forbid sex, this one was male only and took it to an extreme. That's probably why it died out after a while—not enough rabid misogynists to fill the monasteries."

"I can't imagine those teachings going over well with the general population," Quin offered.

"The history of this religious order is a long one, and its followers became more extreme in their beliefs during the last century of its existence," Tiri explained. "Until it died a quiet death, from lack of funding and recruits."

"The bug and mouse crap doesn't bother you?" Lissa asked the twins. She still handled her book as if something might jump out of it at any moment.

"We've seen—and handled—far worse," Tiri sighed. "We don't like

CONNIE SUTTLE

it, but sometimes it's necessary to find what we need. We can take our gloves off and wash our hands later."

"You'd make any archaeologist proud," Lissa said. "I've got a shield around my hands and I still don't want to touch this."

"We have an hour—unless you want to bend time again," Bree warned. Everybody started flipping through pages quickly.

～

Marbool Monarch Hotel
Lissa

"Well, that was a bust," Zaria said as we landed in Nari and Tiri's suite. Mostly what we'd learned was that the religious order was made up of men who found women dirty and distasteful, while singing the praises of the male in every way.

"At least the order died out, if that's any consolation," Nari observed.

"If all men believed in the order's tenets, they'd die out anyway," Quin pointed out. "According to the book I read, sex was certainly off the table."

"And off the floor, the bed, the desk," Zaria teased.

All right—we needed that laugh.

"Now, we need to have a look at the *Book of Kearling*—the real thing," Bree said. "Tonight, when they shut the exhibit down."

"Everybody rest up and get your stealth outfits ready—we're going in," I said.

～

Tiri

I slid the last dagger into my boot sheath before straightening. Nari and I had purchased the dark-brown leather jumpsuits two turns ago, for emergencies. That's the excuse we used, anyway.

We hoped to deserve black leather from a Falchani blademaster someday. Those black leathers were sold only on Falchan and the first

60

set had to be provided by the master—when the student had successfully learned everything and was deserving.

"Ready?" Nari asked.

"Ready," I said. I couldn't hold back the shiver of breathless excitement—as if I'd waited my whole life for this mission.

Nari and I found ourselves shocked that good fortune had come our way—in the guise of powerful queens and others who held talents we couldn't guess at.

It was also a shock that Queens had battled and fought against the forces of darkness—instead of being figureheads, as so many believed.

According to Quin, Queen Reah and her daughter had fought in the battle to retake Kifirin from those who'd usurped the rights and power of the people, who'd been free citizens of the Reth Alliance before the coup.

Nari and I had done as much research as we could on that subject, because it—and High Demons—fascinated us.

"Ready?" Queen Lissa and Breanne appeared in our suite.

"Yes," Nari and I chorused. Breanne folded space to get us into the locked, guarded and alarmed exhibit where the *Book of Kearling* lay.

Zaria

"We're shielded, so we won't trip the alarm," Breanne informed the others. "In a moment, I'll dissolve the clear cover surrounding the book, so we can get to it. The security cameras and recorders will only see an empty room and the book in its usual place. I've dampened the sound, too, so the guards outside won't know we're here."

"Don't worry," she said before Nari could ask a question, "The impenetrable dome over the book will be replaced and all will be as it was, once we're done."

"Then let's get to work," Lissa said. I raised my hands and dissolved the clear barrier around the book in a flurry of winking sparks.

Lissa

All of us wore cotton gloves this time, and the only difference I noticed was that the real book was completely intact—all of it, with no signs of mouse nibbles, damage from bugs or any other thing. It had survived on a monastery shelf, surrounded by other books that had certainly not fared as well.

Then, it had passed from one institute to another through many centuries, long before book preservation practices were even considered. I marveled that it had survived so well.

"You think whoever added that last section left a spell to keep vermin and decay away from the book, so it would be preserved intact?" I asked as Nari and Tiri carefully lifted a page to turn it.

"It could very well be," Bree agreed as she looked over Nari's shoulder at the book. "I can't explain it otherwise, and it's like Nefrigar says—every time I try to find the spells or anything else other than what's printed in ink on these pages, it's as if it knows to conceal itself from prying power."

"A tricky spell, to say the least," Zaria shook her head.

"And a successful one," Kiarra agreed.

My head jerked up at the sound of a scuffle outside the exhibit room. We were locked inside, but it sounded as if the guards at the door were having problems.

"What the fuck?" Breanne's head jerked up and turned toward the door.

"Want me," I began, ready to go outside the room to see what the problem was.

I didn't have time to finish my sentence. The door burst open, and several hundred members of the Brotherhood of the Dark Moon ran in, like cockroaches swarming through a kitchen after the lights were turned out.

Quin

Under normal circumstances, someone would have screamed or ran at this turn of events.

The women in this room—all ten of us—did neither.

Nari and Tiri pulled weapons from hidden sheaths in their clothing, prepared to fight as the Brothers of the Dark Moon swarmed into the exhibit. Eerily—the Brothers were silent as well, but it wasn't because they'd intended that.

No.

Each of them were controlled by something else.

What are they doing? Kiarra sent as she, Devin and Grace *Pulled* in blades to defend themselves. For now, Breanne held a shield around all of us, preventing the Brothers from reaching our small group, which was clustered around the book.

They're trying to reach the book, Zaria replied. I turned swiftly in her direction. She was glowing softly golden in the dim light of the exhibit.

Everybody ready? Breanne asked.

Lower the shield, Zaria said. *Only kill if they attack you,* she warned.

What happened? I was surprised to hear Nari's mindspeech.

The book just called them in, Breanne rumbled in mindspeech. *As we're women, we're so far beneath its notice, we may as well not be here,* she added. *Shield coming down.*

Now.

That's when, as Queen Lissa would say, all hell broke loose.

CHAPTER 5

*L*issa

I wanted to scream—and not stop screaming, as hundreds of thousands of cockroaches, all hidden within the ink adorning pages of an ancient book, flowed out of its leaves faster than rushing water.

I almost gagged when the Brothers of the Dark Moon opened their mouths so they could be filled with escaping insects.

Can't we do something? Kiarra didn't sound as if her stomach were completely steady as insects disappeared down male gullets.

Not yet, Breanne held up a hand. *We have to wait until the last one is out.*

Gross, Devin remarked as more and more cockroaches spilled out of the book and swarmed up the Brothers' robes until they found an open mouth.

By that time, the room had filled to capacity with Brothers, and still more came. Breanne was forced to enlarge the room with power —I knew she didn't want any of the Brothers leaving the room again, just to make room for more.

She, Kiarra and I had put up a barrier shield around the entire building, too, so that none could escape, once the last roach had left the book.

I didn't know exactly why, yet, but there was a reason. I hoped I could keep the contents of my stomach where they were until that moment came. Frankly, I was beginning to have my doubts.

After all, I'd seen the Ra'Ak's kiss and that was as ugly and nauseating as you could get—until I saw this.

How many fucking bugs can that book hold? Kiarra asked. The flow of insects hadn't slowed down even a little.

Need help? Charles' mindspeech reached all of us.

No! was chorused right back at him, from ten different female minds.

Just checking. He sounded as if he were smirking, the rat.

At that moment, the last of the bugs exited the book, like water turned off at the tap. Every Brother of the Dark Moon was now filled to the brim with cockroaches, and the room had grown so large I couldn't see into the darkened corners of it.

The Master of the Dark Moon had called in all of his members—likely after being ordered to do so by the one who as yet hadn't left the book behind.

Get ready, Breanne warned.

The father of all cockroaches poked his head from the crease between pages, as if he'd stuffed himself into the spine and only now chose to leave his hiding space.

Fuck. No wonder the information hid from us so well, Breanne's voice hissed into our minds. Just like cockroaches can disappear into the walls, these had been moving around, from one word to the next—from one page to the next, all this time, so we'd never guess the truth.

You know what they say, Zaria said as the large cockroach continued to leverage himself out of his tight, hiding place.

What's that? Kiarra asked, distractedly. All eyes, as expected, were on our fearless cockroach leader.

That when the apocalypse comes, all that will survive are the cockroaches, she explained.

While Zaria sent mindspeak, she'd begun to glow brighter. The

Brothers, whose mouths were now closed to carry their cockroach passengers safely out of the exhibit, began to hum.

They were singing to their master; the last to emerge from the pages of an ancient book. He continued his efforts to remove his body from the tight space he occupied—like a deadly creature hatching from the vilest of eggs.

How's the search going? Breanne pointed her question to Zaria.

It can take a little time—stall them for me, all right? Try not to kill any humans while you're at it.

Understood.

The master cockroach pulled himself completely out of the book's spine and dropped to the floor.

He changed.

Became taller—larger—until he was taller than the tallest of the Brothers surrounding him.

Still, he acted as if he hadn't seen any of us. *I've shielded us individually*, Breanne said. *He doesn't know that we're here. Neither do the Brothers. I don't know how we can ensure that remains true, once we keep them from leaving.*

I have an idea, I said.

What's that?

Just keep them from leaving. Let me take care of the rest, I replied.

Still searching, Zaria informed us. I had no idea what she was searching for—perhaps a recipe for the best bug bomb ever, which wouldn't kill the humans involved.

I hoped she hurried—I had no idea how much power the master cockroach had, and damn, he was *huge*.

Breanne

When Lissa said she had an idea, I had no idea she meant *that* idea.

I'd placed a conical, invisible shield around each of us while more cockroaches than I'd ever dreamed existed ran out of a book as if a giant can of bug spray was chasing them.

Lissa took all my conical shields and turned them into pinball bumpers. Now, every time a Brother of the Dark Moon bumped into one, it tossed him away like a steel ball smacked by an aluminum bat.

That wasn't the bad part.

Oh, no.

The bad part? After a few moments of Brothers getting smacked away from shields, they, by a law of physics or something, bumped into other Brothers, who, in turn, became humanoid pinball bumpers.

Even that wasn't the worst part, although it was emphatically unnerving to see Brothers filled to the brim with cockroaches banging off each other like thousands of ping-pong balls in a violent tornado.

And, as you may have guessed, those Brothers, when the air was knocked out of their lungs with a whoosh—began spitting cockroaches everywhere.

That was the bad part.

Men were banging into shields and into each other, hundreds of times per minute, and every collision resulted in another spray of insects—against walls, on floors, each other, our shields—even the ceiling.

Watching someone else vomiting always triggers my own gag reflex, and let me tell you, I've never had to work so hard to keep from barfing as I did while watching two thousand men or more whacking into each other and spewing bugs.

Some of those cockroaches attempted to climb back up the Brothers' robes, to take their place inside again, only to get knocked off or spewed out.

For Pete's sake, I shouted mentally at Zaria.

He hasn't revealed himself, yet, she informed me.

That forced my attention back to the master cockroach, who stood beside the stand holding the book, gazing at the chaos around him as if mesmerized.

I kept watching, mesmerized a little myself, as he lifted a foreleg. Just like that, all the Brothers went still and stopped spewing cockroaches.

The language he spoke—whatever cockroach-ey thing he used, the Brothers appeared to understand, as they gathered around him, prepared to allow the crawling insects inside them again.

Please say this is almost over, Lissa begged.

I have this, Zaria announced, before releasing the shield I'd placed around her and becoming visible to all present, including Master cockroach and all his minions, insect and humanoid.

Just when you think it can't get any worse, Kiarra's voice breathed into my mind as the Master cockroach's head morphed into a humanoid one.

"I should have known," the humanoid head spoke, now—in an ancient version of the dialect spoken on Marbool a thousand years or more in the past.

"Known what?" Zaria glowed a little brighter, bringing Master cockroach into sharper focus.

"That a foolish woman would attempt to bring us down. We are the master race, have you not seen it? We exist. We will always exist. It was only a matter of time before we developed power of our own. You are nothing. Get out of my way or I'll kill you now instead of watching you and others like you die a long, excruciating death."

"You really bought into that whole *male-is-everything* tenet, didn't you?" Zaria lifted an eyebrow. The Larentii was coming out in her, although she hadn't changed, yet.

"You cannot destroy me," he laughed. "I have more power than you can ever dream of. Now stand aside, or you will die."

"You'll have to get past me, first." Zaria changed, then, and became eight feet of blue-skinned, white-winged Larentii.

"What is this?" Master cockroach hissed. "Never mind, your power is still puny next to mine. You are a woman, and any woman will always be less than a male—even one of a different species."

"Damn, dude, that's some ego you have, there," Zaria frowned at him.

Oh lord, Lissa sighed. While Zaria and master cockroach were having their standoff, the roaches that had been knocked out of the

Brothers were now crawling back in. It was bad enough to witness that once—twice was way too much.

Can we move this along a little faster? I whined at Zaria.

Turns out, I hadn't needed to prod her—master cockroach was done talking, or so it appeared.

His head went back to being that of a cockroach, and whatever he chittered or clicked convinced the Brothers to attempt to attack Zaria.

She'd shielded herself from them, but it was still disconcerting to watch as the brothers piled atop each other, until they'd built a mound of bodies up and over her dome-shaped shield.

Master cockroach, if he'd been humanoid enough, would have crossed at least two sets of legs over his thorax and contemplated the conundrum that faced him—that of a woman who held power.

Frankly, I hadn't attempted to read him before this; I had no desire to look into the mental workings of an insect.

What I saw in a few seconds would have filled half a library of books.

That's when Zaria apparently had enough of humanoid, roach-carrying bodies attempting to smother her from the outside.

Golden light and Brothers' bodies exploded outward, reenacting the scenes of roaches spewing out of male mouths like projectile vomiting while crashing into walls or onto floors.

Oh, puke, Lissa grimaced.

That's when Quin stepped in to do what she could.

Any animal—or insect, too, I learned, wouldn't or couldn't resist her call. She called to the cockroaches, and they responded.

Oh, no, Grace moaned as cockroaches began swarming out of mouths and running for the walls.

I shielded every micron of space so they couldn't crawl into, underneath or through anything in the exhibit room.

"What are you doing to my people?' the humanoid head was back atop the cockroach master's body, and he shouted at Zaria.

"I didn't do that," she shrugged.

"You are nothing, and I will take my people and go," he took a step forward.

"You and your people are going nowhere," Zaria said, holding out a hand, palm upward.

"What is that?" Master cockroach blinked temporarily humanoid eyes at the small, gold square at the center of Zaria's palm.

"It's you," she glanced at her palm, then back to him.

"I am here," he snapped at her, tapping his thorax with a foreleg. "It is time for me and my people to leave. We have things to do, and this world to take for ourselves."

I felt it, then—the power he was gathering to himself.

Oh, crap, Lissa sent.

I suppose, if you were a cockroach born with unusual power, who'd gathered more power the longer he'd nibbled on dead monks during a three-year drought when food was scarce, you couldn't help but absorb some of what they were—enough to attract a rogue god, who saw that in the future, the end of his fellows would come.

Sometime, before the monk who'd written most of the *Book of Kearling* died, a rogue god had gone looking for the most unlikely place to hide, to save his life.

He'd found the absolute experts at hiding—cockroaches.

Finding one that held power, well, that was just a bonus.

"You will not hinder me," master cockroach thundered, and just for good measure, blew the roof off the entire building.

Even with my shields around the place, he'd done that.

Who knew it had started raining outside?

He's gathering power to take himself and the others out of here, Kiarra shouted mentally.

That's when we all went still and silent.

I'd never heard that voice before—the one that came from Zaria's mouth.

It was neither male nor female, and it held the dark rumble of metal upon metal.

"You will not continue," the voice said. Zaria's eyes had gone completely gold—like the metal turned liquid—as she stared at master cockroach-slash-rogue god-slash insect king.

Perhaps he felt his danger, then.

Zaria still held the small, gold square on her palm.

Master cockroach leapt forward to snatch it away from her.

As any Larentii can do, Zaria separated the gold square's particles before he could take it, the winking sparks flying upward and mingling with the concurrently dissipating sparks of master cockroach.

Until he was gone.

"And now, I *Change What Was*," I announced to a wet, stormy sky, and everything turned white for just a moment.

CHAPTER 6

A vendor
    Breanne

"You're not going to tell us, are you?" Ashe asked.

"Nope."

He and Charles stood at the windows of Ashe's SouthStar palace, gazing at miles of gishi fruit trees below the hill where the palace stood.

They'd asked me about Zaria. About what she'd done and what she'd become.

As long as I lived, I wouldn't reveal that secret, and neither would any other woman who'd stood with her that night.

Too bad she hadn't been what she currently was before the God Wars. That might have made things a little easier on all of us.

Or not.

That's when I understood something vital. When she'd taken the metal library into herself, she'd forced the fusion, to allow everything to survive.

With a few exceptions, of course. A cockroach god was one of those exceptions. Somewhere within her, without a doubt, there was a small, gold square for each of us, including the Mighty.

I felt we were in good hands.

"What about Nari and Tiri?" Charles asked, turning back to me.

"Well, I introduced them to Salidar. He'll be training them to be Falchani-style blademasters," I shrugged. "After that, we may find some work for them to do."

"They really are relic wardens?" Ashe asked.

"Nefrigar says so. I'd say we haven't seen the last of those two." Just the thought of it made me smile. "They're nulls, you know—most wizards, warlocks and mundane power wielders won't be able to put any sort of spell on them. It's how their family has nullified powerful objects in the past. I suspect that somewhere, far in their past, they have High Demon ancestry. Having said that, however, I think that this time—with a rogue god inhabiting the *Book of Kearling*, they didn't have a way to combat or nullify that."

"So—the *Book of Kearling*?" Charles lifted an eyebrow at me.

"Is, in all appearances, just as it has always been. Once the rogue god cockroach and his minions exited the book, the parts invisible to humanoid eyes also disappeared. The only copy of the book containing those images is the one in the Larentii Archives."

"What about the Brothers of the Dark Moon?"

"All whole, roach-free and back to their old ways of spreading outrageous rumors of doom and gloom. They have no idea how close they came to being mere vessels for cockroach overlords."

"What are your plans, now?" Ashe asked.

"I need a vacation," I sighed.

The End

ROSE OF THE PEAKS

CHAPTER 1

Queen's Palace, Le-Ath Veronis
Lissa

I watched as Renée gathered the envelopes from my desk —they all contained Christmas wishes for the vampires who celebrated the holiday in Lissia.

Many of them were from old Earth and held their traditions dearly —and tightly—as only a vampire could. Tony joked once that they'd let go of the holiday when someone pulled it from their cold, dead ashes.

I'd smacked him on the shoulder for his impertinence.

Mostly because I celebrate Christmas, too.

Every year, at the appropriate time (which varied, because Le-Ath Veronis' year wasn't exactly equivalent to Earth's), I'd sign cards and buy gifts. This year, Christmas was two weeks away. I'd already bought gifts; signed cards would now be sent to those vampires who'd appreciate them most.

What is Montrose waiting for? Rigo, who'd sat patiently in a corner, tapping his comp-vid and doing secret spy-stuff, no doubt, looked at me when Renée left my private study.

Montrose was Renée's vampire parent—and he was in love with her.

As she was in love with him.

Except lately, she'd begun to lose her hope that he'd ever make a move to change things between them—from the parent-child dynamic to the more intimate variety.

Her training period was over shortly after we'd celebrated Christmas last year. In all those months, he hadn't said a word or given her hope of any kind. Sure, he'd shown up regularly to take her out on a lunch break to New Fangled or another destination, but nothing else.

I have no idea what he's waiting for, I responded to Rigo's question. Any other man—or vampire—would have asked her to marry him by now. *It's as if he's holding her at arm's length for some unknown reason,* I added.

"You know," I said aloud to Rigo, "my mother, whenever I or someone else wasn't moving fast enough to get something done, would say, *what are you waiting for—Christmas?*"

Rigo lifted an eyebrow and studied me intently. "I'm sure that has a deeper meaning than the one I'm assigning to it," he replied, his words dry.

"Don't make me put coal in your stocking," I pointed a finger at him.

"I have plenty of stockings, and have no need for coal. That is an ancient and no longer viable method of producing energy."

"Well, aren't we Mr. Encyclopedia today," I grumped.

"Tiessa, I merely wait for you to finish your thoughts, as I intend to take you to New Fangled. I hear they have decorated for this holiday you obviously love, and ah, Christmas carols are being played."

He said Christmas carols as if he wasn't sure what they were, exactly. "You love me," I accused, pointing at him again.

"Of course I love you, but why are you saying it like this?"

"Because you don't even know what a Christmas carol is, but you're willing to suffer through it just for me."

"I hoped there would be no suffering involved," his words were dry. "Although Anthony certainly thinks there will be."

"I doubt Flavio will have *Grandma Got Run Over by a Reindeer* playing on a loop," I muttered. "Most Christmas carols are nice—even if you don't understand the language."

"I understand English perfectly." Now he sounded just a smidge away from outrageous indignation.

If there were something new to learn or know, then Rigo would be second in line to learn or research it, after his mentor, Kell. No doubt his grasp of the English language was better than mine—by a long way.

But why would I tell him that? It was more fun to tease him.

"Are we folding or driving?" I asked.

"I thought a drive would be nice."

"Lead the way." I gestured toward the door.

Five minutes later, after we'd walked through half the palace to get to the private side door, we discovered it was raining. Water dripped off the car beneath the porte cochère, as the comesula driver jumped from the driver's seat to open a door for us.

"Oh, I wish it was snow," I breathed, finding that my breath blew out in a puff of white. "When did it get cold?" I turned to Rigo.

"While you surely had your nose buried in work," he shrugged.

"You knew it was cold and you didn't tell me?"

"I will wrap you in my arms—and also in the coat that is waiting on the seat for you."

"What about you?" I turned my face up to his. A slight smile lurked about his mouth, but try getting more than that from an older-than-dirt vampire, especially if he isn't playing along.

Taking my elbow, he ushered me into the back seat of the vehicle, where a pile of coats almost blocked the view from the opposite window. He'd gone through my closet and pulled out several coats, so I could take my pick.

I noticed there was one for him, too, when I reached the bottom of the pile.

"You must have been the best King Hraede ever had," I pulled out his coat and handed it to him. "You think of everything."

"It is wise in all things to be prepared for all things." He did grin, this time. The hover-limo was warm inside as the driver pulled away from the palace, but Rigo still held me against him as we nestled into the back seat together.

~

Montrose

Snow—a rare occurrence in Lissia, had been forecast. Already, rain was freezing on limbs and twigs as I gazed out a window. On Earth, Christmas would come in two weeks. I always marked that time with a great sadness, and generally put away the Queen's Christmas cards without reading them.

Of course I thanked her every time, but the old holiday was just too painful to me. Too, snow in Lissia was a far cry from what I'd seen in my final dwelling place as a human, long ago in France.

Still, the scent in the air—of cold, moisture and frost—sent me back to a much older time. Not many knew that I was the youngest member of the Vampire Council on Earth. Most of them were more than a thousand years old when the Council was formed. I'd been vampire for four hundred years when one of the original members was killed.

Still, Wlodek had sought me out himself, depending upon my desire to treat all fairly as a deciding factor in making me a member of that governing body.

He knew some things about me—through my sire.

He didn't know everything.

Here in Lissia, the terrain was relatively flat. I'd seen snow grace housetops and the dome of the Queen's palace. *Beautiful,* most of my compatriots would declare. And it was.

Nothing Lissia offered could compare to the snow surrounding Montsegur, on a bright morning after a heavy fall. The light would fall so intensely upon that whiteness that it could blind anyone not prepared for it.

Yes, I'd received the Queen's blood, just as my adopted child Renée had received it, to make the turn. I could go to the sunlit half of the planet if I wanted—live there, too, if I wanted. It would only remind me of my younger days, however, so I chose to stay where I was.

They'd razed the castle on Montsegur afterward, and built a fortress over it, as if it had never been. With a sigh, I turned away from my window as the first few white flakes sailed past. The fragile crystals would fail to survive against the water already on the ground, and would disappear as if they, too, had never been.

Renée

Sometimes, I wondered why I'd been brought to Le-Ath Veronis. I wasn't born here, like many thought. Queen Lissa knew my background, as did Montrose, but not many others were aware.

I'd been sick, too, when I came, and that was a violation of the rules governing Le-Ath Veronis. Those rules were designed to prevent anyone from seeking to extend their lives by becoming vampire.

I understood the reasoning behind those rules; if they didn't exist, eventually the wealthy would pay to be turned and the planet would be overrun by those who never should have been turned to begin with.

Only the worthy are turned, Queen Lissa said often enough. Comesuli were carefully considered when the time was right, and decisions were made, all without their knowledge or input.

One simply couldn't campaign to become vampire, like they did for a political office. They were either found worthy or they weren't, and that's how things went.

I was dying on Avendor—I knew it and my family knew it. They surrounded my bedside at the hospital near our home, waiting for the inevitable to come. I'd slept, then awakened at another hospital—here on Le-Ath Veronis.

CONNIE SUTTLE

Someone had come—I couldn't recall whom—and he'd asked me if I wanted to live. That memory remains murky; I can't remember anything else of it, except that I'd whispered *yes* to the question.

Days later, eleven to be exact, I'd wakened to find Montrose hovering over me, a welcoming smile on his face and a bottle of blood substitute in his hand, to feed me.

His arms had wrapped around me as I shivered and drank.

It's one of my fondest memories—his tight embrace and soft, encouraging words in a language I didn't understand.

My learning period was long past, and I'd hoped that he and I —*well*. That had turned into a foolish hope. He remained the same while I, feeling rejected, had begun to pull away.

For self-preservation.

The heart can only survive so much pain before it hardens against the source of it. The only reason I still had lunch with him now and then was the memory I kept—of him holding me and speaking softly against my hair.

That was the Montrose I dreamed about—the Montrose I wanted to keep forever. Not the one who kept his secrets away from me, and refused to tell me of his past life. I'd asked him twice about it. The second time, he became angry and told me never to ask again.

So I didn't.

"Here are the Christmas cards." I set the box containing the snowy white envelopes in front of the vampire who ran the Queen's mail room. The counter between us was the first thing I'd seen upon entering, as always.

Jones, the Chief Mail Clerk, always left whatever he was doing behind a wall of shelves and cubbyholes, to arrive at the counter as if hounds were chasing him.

"Ah," he nodded before lifting the box and setting it on a shelf behind him. "Those will be delivered tomorrow morning. Tell the Queen I will see to it myself."

"I'll tell her. Uh, Jones?" I asked before he turned away.

"What is it, Miss Renée?" He always called me that. Sometimes it made me giggle.

"I was just wondering—if you have anyone special in your life."

"Upon occasion I have a drink with this one or that at New Fangled, or one of the casinos," he said. "But I don't consider any one of them *special*, as you put it. Why do you ask?"

He thought I was coming on to him. I wasn't—I knew he liked men. I merely wanted advice from someone who had experience with relationships.

I'd never had a relationship. I'd been born sick, and eventually, the disease had taken me down—or almost. Vampirism cures anything, if you survive the turn.

"I was just looking for advice," I sighed. "That's all."

The look of sympathy on his face told me everything—he and everybody else in the palace probably knew I loved Montrose, and that it was a hopeless cause.

"Thank you anyway." I turned and left him standing there, staring after me and *feeling sorry for my ass*, as Queen Lissa would say.

∾

New Fangled

Lissa

A quartet made up of old-Earth vampires sang *Angels We Have Heard on High*, as I twirled spaghetti on a fork. Before I ordered it, I considered that I could end up wearing sauce on my top, but I really wanted spaghetti, and I was powerful enough to remove spaghetti sauce stains from my clothes if I wanted.

"This is really good," I told Rigo, before stuffing spaghetti in my mouth.

"The music or the food?" he lifted an eyebrow.

Both, I sent, because my mouth was full.

"I suppose it grows on you," he turned toward the quartet. "Did angels truly have wings, like the Avii?"

"I don't think anybody has wings like the Avii," I said. "Besides, the jury is still out, although the artists almost always portrayed angels as having wings."

"I have perused several books on Earth art," Rigo nodded. "Perhaps it was a way of designating them as angels, just as halos were employed to indicate the divinity of the individual."

"Or maybe they just wanted to paint wings," I said. "In a few of those old paintings, where people were draped in ten thousand yards of cloth, it showed off the artist's ability to draw or paint drapery, as well as being an indication of wealth or decadence."

"They were not dressed in ten thousand yards of cloth. You exaggerate."

"Honey, that's exaggeration draped in sarcasm, and you should know that about me already. Why are you acting all surprised now?"

"*Draped* in sarcasm? I see what you did there. Amusing."

"You don't sound amused."

"Ah. I am also capable of employing sarcasm. As a method of self-defense, you understand."

"You think I'm attacking you?"

"I wish you were. In a physical sense, of course."

I racked my brain to recall when Rigo and I had last been—oh. "Honey, why didn't you say that before I ate a plate full of spaghetti?"

"Because you were hungry."

"And now I smell like garlic and tomato sauce."

"You can brush your teeth—and then come shopping with me this afternoon."

"Ohhhhh—I can look for a few last-minute stocking stuffers for Wayne and Wynter."

"I thought you might be interested."

"You're the best," I said, scraping up the last of my spaghetti. He laughed, and that was worth a lot to me.

Renée

"We're going Christmas shopping this afternoon," Grant whooshed into my small office and announced. "Lissa just said we could have the afternoon off. That includes you, worky-pants."

"Worky-pants?" I made a face at Grant. His nicknames usually didn't convey confidence in the one so-named.

"Come on," Heathe coaxed, walking in to join Grant. "You haven't bought the Queen a gift yet, now have you?"

"No." I hung my head. She always gave us things—and money, too—she called it our Christmas bonus, and it was more than generous.

We always gave a small token in return—but it had to be well-thought out and something she wouldn't think to get for herself. Often, it was desk accessories or a new tea mug with "World's Best Queen," on it or something.

Her favorite mug had come from her Falchani mates. It read, "Itty-Bitty-Pants," and I'd thought it scandalous the first time I'd seen it.

I learned it was a joke sometime later, and besides, Drake and Drew were more than amazing—and funny—and handsome.

Queen Lissa had mates running out her ears—by her own admission. I couldn't get one, even, and that's all I wanted—just one.

Montrose. The man with sensuous lips, a pensive gaze and brown hair that he kept carefully styled unless the day was windy. I loved those days, because his hair would be mussed ever so slightly, revealing a rugged handsomeness that I'd come to love.

"Let me get my coat," I mumbled at Grant, tearing myself away from visions of Montrose on better days.

Lissa

"The snow is starting to stick," I breathed. I felt like jumping up and down, I was so excited. I wanted snow. Lots of it—snow crunching beneath the boots I kept in my closet that I seldom wore because there wasn't any need for them.

"Tiessa, I wish I could take credit for this weather, but alas, I cannot." Rigo drew the collar of my coat up to keep me warmer as we trudged toward one of my favorite toy shops.

Already, a fine layer of white stuff covered open areas, while flakes swirled and eddied around shops and casinos in Casino City. The only thing missing was Christmas music, but I couldn't expect everybody to adopt my favorite holiday.

"Some planets celebrate midwinter," I said.

"Except that midwinter is not consistent from planet to planet," Rigo pointed out. "In all the worlds belonging to both Alliances, you could find a celebration of some kind every day, if you were so minded to take the time and trouble for it."

Rigo held the shop door open so I could enter—somewhere behind us and being as discreet as possible—were four palace guards who would be watching for anyone approaching me with more than a benign intent.

Not that I couldn't take care of myself, or didn't have a shield around Rigo and me that only the Mighty Hand could break. Having guards was standard protocol. I'd gotten used to it, and Rigo would have removed heads if the effort wasn't made.

The vampire clerk near the door almost gasped when I entered the toy shop—he was new but recognized me anyway. Rigo's upheld hand told the man not to make a fuss; we didn't want every tourist in the store to know that the Queen of Le-Ath Veronis was there. They'd want selfies with the Queen, and I wanted to shop for my kids.

Humming *Good King Wenceslas*, I headed for the age-appropriate shelves to find something for Wayne and Wynter, that might withstand the wear and tear a young werewolf would give it.

Montrose

The snow falling on Lissia and Casino City, against the odds, was sticking. A pale covering of fluff now lay across my front lawn. Renée would likely take joy in it—where she was from on Avendor, it was nearly always warm, and she'd not seen snow until she came to Le-Ath Veronis.

Snow.

So many memories tied into it, both good and bad.

That day on Montsegur, only a day before Christmas, invaded my memory against my will. It had been snowing, then, and darkness was coming fast as we prepared to leave.

By a hidden passage, we'd slip past the troops surrounding us in a siege that had lasted more than six months already. This plan had been laid carefully, although we'd hoped the weather would be better.

I and six others were selected to guard three *perfecti* and the treasure they'd bear away from the siege, to prevent it falling into the hands of our tormentors. If they found us, they'd take the valuables for themselves—and destroy us and the precious writings we carried.

The *perfecti* were passive and abhorred violence. They held no weapons to defend themselves. It fell upon us, their knight-protectors, to keep them from harm.

"Phillipe," I can still hear my commander's voice that night. "Take the rear—with Anselme. Make sure we aren't followed. If they find us, buy time for us to get away."

"It will be done."

We'd carry the treasure on our backs, divided between us, until we met with villagers at the bottom of the mountain. They'd have horses waiting for us, to make a swifter journey away from the mountain.

Until then, we'd be going through the forest along a downward trail, so steep it was difficult to keep one's footing. This hidden trail was chosen in an attempt to conceal our escape from those who watched the mountain. Traveling down the mountain on a snowy, dark night wasn't ideal, but it was necessary.

"Phillipe?"

I heard her voice, too—calling out as we began our journey—away from Montsegur.

Away from the woman I loved.

"Be safe and return to me," she added softly. I couldn't turn to look —there were tears in her voice. I should have married her before I left. Perhaps it would have convinced her to live afterward.

The chime from my front door sounded, interrupting my thoughts. I discovered I was trembling, not from cold, but from the memory of it.

"I have it," my comesula servant called out.

"Thank you, Weff," I said, grateful for the interruption. I couldn't bury myself in these memories and past griefs. It was useless to do so. Only heartache would come of it, as I'd felt it many times in the past.

"A delivery," Weff appeared at my elbow in my private study.

"What is this?" I accepted the small, gold-colored bag carefully. It appeared fragile to me, and had been hand-carried to my home, that was quite obvious.

"The one delivering it said there's a note inside the bag," Weff pointed to the corner of paper peeking over the edge of the tiny sack.

I withdrew the note and unfolded it.

Do not open until Christmas Eve, it read.

There was no signature.

"What do you suppose that means?" Weff's voice held puzzlement.

"No idea," I said. "Lay it on my desk. I'll see about it later."

"Of course." Weff took the bag to my desk, then headed toward the door. I heard his footsteps retreat from my study as I turned back to the snow falling outside.

Renée

"There's a small art gallery inside the Chessman," Grant said, leading the way after we'd left the comp-vid and electronics store behind empty-handed. "Maybe we can find something Lissa would like in there."

The casino in question was two blocks away, so we pulled the collars of our coats up and walked through falling snow to get there.

"Snow is great when you're inside watching it," Heathe rumbled. "I need a new scarf," he added.

"Vampires aren't supposed to feel cold," Grant reminded him.

"This vampire does," Heathe snarked back.

By that time, we'd reached the main entrance of the Chessman, where two doormen rushed to open the doors for us.

"Thank you," I smiled at them—both were vampires.

"Merry Christmas, Dirke," Grant told the one on the left.

"Merry Christmas to you, Grant," Dirke actually grinned. That meant Dirke was from Earth, just as Grant was. Heathe settled for nodding at the other vampire—whom nobody recognized, apparently.

We walked into the grand, circular entry that led to a reception desk, the concierge and a members' club kiosk. The tile-covered path straight ahead led to restaurants, shopping and other amusements—while walking through the casino, of course.

The Chessman was all about understated elegance and good taste, unlike many of the other casinos. Every time I walked into it, I always felt underdressed for the occasion.

"I smell gingerbread," Grant breathed and quickened his pace. Heathe and I practically ran to keep up with him—he was headed for cookie bliss, in my opinion.

Sure enough, we reached a cookie and sweets kiosk, where fresh gingerbread cookies were lying on a tray, waiting for people to buy and taste.

"I want a dozen," Grant said right away.

"Don't hog them," Heathe mumbled, staring at the delicious, vaguely humanoid-shaped confections.

After Grant's dozen cookies were counted out, there were only six remaining. Heathe and I took three each, emptying the tray.

"We'll have a fresh batch in about an hour," the clerk informed us as we took boxes of carefully packaged cookies from her.

"We'll be back," Grant grinned before continuing our trek to the art gallery.

"This is nice," Grant lifted a hand-made case for sunglasses. Yes, there were other, electronic ways to protect your eyes in bright light, but sunglasses as a fashion accessory had experienced a rebirth, and now everyone was attempting to cash in on the fad.

"Lissa loves her sunglasses," Grant said, checking the wall-mounted comp for the price. "Yes," he said, once the price popped onto the screen. "Less than two hundred credits? I'm done." He skipped toward the desk to pay.

"Why can't we get that lucky?" Heathe grumbled as we sorted through paperweights, doo-dads and tchotchkes, as Queen Lissa referred to them. Mostly they were useless knick-knacks that cluttered up shelves and required too much dusting—also as she described them.

"None of this will work," I shook my head at all of it.

"There are more cubbies to go," Heathe said, pulling me farther into the gallery. We rounded a corner, where small sculptures lay on stands short and tall, to properly display them.

As I scanned the items, I looked past a shorter wall on the opposite side—to see the wall at the back of the gallery. There, displayed alone, was a near-life-size painting of a man with a sword at his hip.

I gasped and left Heathe behind in the cubby, hissing my name.

It couldn't be, I told myself as I came closer to the painting. The man, dressed in a rough leather vest and dark trousers, had a hand on the pommel of his sword as he stood atop a rocky outcropping and gazed upon the terrain below.

Dusk was falling around him, and snow blew his hair awry.

This was the Montrose of my dreams—the man in my heart. His face held grim purpose, as if he were contemplating a difficult task ahead. His sword and heavy boots indicated, perhaps, that a battle lay ahead of him, in treacherous weather.

I wanted it.

Knew it could cost far too much for me to afford it.

"That came in earlier today—we don't get many paintings from this artist," the gallery curator now stood beside me. That made the price go up by thousands in my head. "He's very talented, don't you think?" The curator continued.

"It's amazing," I breathed, unable to take my eyes away.

"It's four thousand credits," he told me.

"I can't," I hung my head, defeated. One or two thousand, and I'd scrimp and save to cover the cost. This was twice that, and may as well have been hung on an airless moon, somewhere, far from my mundane reach.

"Here's the artist, now." I jerked my head up at the curator's words.

"Hello," the tall, sandy-haired man held out a hand to me. "Are you interested in the warrior I painted?"

"Is that what it's called?" I squeaked.

"What would you call it?" he asked gently.

"Montrose," I whispered.

"Ah. You know someone like that?" he nodded toward the painting.

"Yes." I dropped my eyes again. "It's beautiful, and I'd buy it if I could."

"If I drop the price, will you be interested?"

"I can't pay half what it's worth," I admitted, my cheeks turning hot.

"I'll sell it to you, here and now, for fifteen hundred. You must say yes now, or the deal will be withdrawn."

"Yes. Yes, please," I begged.

"There is one condition," the artist held up a hand. "You must allow it to hang in the gallery here for eleven days, to show the work and invite future commissions. Then you may have it delivered."

"Yes, of course," I breathed, my hands clasped against my chest to hide their trembling.

"I'll draw up the sale," the curator smiled and led me toward the desk.

CHAPTER 2

*L*issa

Is that—that's Heathe and Grant," I said, slipping my arm into Rigo's just outside the art gallery in Adam Chessman's casino.

"They're probably buying you gifts," Rigo lifted an eyebrow at me.

"They'll be spending too much on me in there," I declared. "Come on, let's go see what they're up to."

Grant saw us the moment we walked in. He held a small, gallery bag in his hand—too late to interfere with that purchase, I suppose.

They were waiting at the sales desk when Rigo and I joined them. "Doing some Christmas shopping?" I asked, grinning at both.

"Why, uh, no," Grant hid the bag behind his back.

"Right," I said, sounding just as disbelieving as I truly was.

"We're waiting on Renée," Heathe said. "She just bought a huge painting in the back of the gallery."

"Seriously? I've never known her to be interested in artwork before. Is it a gift for someone?"

"No—I ah, think this one is for her," Grant coughed.

"We need to see this," I told Rigo, who followed me quickly toward the back of the store. We stopped dead the moment I caught sight of

Lynx—and Renée—in front of a painting that Lynx had obviously done.

Even without Lynx's presence, I'd recognize his work anywhere; he was more than talented and his paintings—whenever he did them, were in high demand.

"It's Montrose," Rigo sighed as he gazed at the large, framed portrait of a tall man on a mountain.

"Oh, my gosh," I breathed as I took in the scene before me. Something—and someone—was at work here, and while I could speculate, I didn't want to. This was a story unfolding before our eyes, I think.

"Let's go," I turned, forcing Rigo to turn with me. We marched right out of the gallery, without Renée knowing that we'd even come.

"That's right," I spoke with the gallery curator two hours later on my comp-vid. "I'd like the painting charged to me, after it's delivered to her. It's a gift. If I'd known it was there, I'd have bought it for her anyway."

"But the price will be the full price if you purchase it, my Queen," the curator said, sounding apologetic. "The artist agreed to reduce the price only for this customer."

"No problem—charge me full price," I said. I'd have a talk with Lynx about all this—after Christmas.

"Shall I send the record of the refund to the palace at the appropriate time?" he asked.

"Please—and thank you for going to this much trouble for me."

"It is never a difficulty when it's for the lovely Queen of Le-Ath Veronis. Your assistant, Renée, asked for the painting to be delivered to the palace—shall I follow her instructions?"

"Absolutely. Nothing is changed, except the method of payment."

"Lynx," I whispered after ending the communication, "We *will* have a talk about all this. After Christmas."

Renée

"I'm afraid I have bad news," the gallery curator informed me. I watched his face on my comp-vid—he looked pale and worried.

"What is it?" Yes, I was at my desk, three days before the Queen's Christmas holiday, when the painting was scheduled to be delivered.

"Your painting has disappeared," the man said, his voice wobbling. "Nothing else was taken, only that, but as it's hung in the gallery for several days, we've had many inquiries about it. Some were more than disappointed when they learned it was already sold."

"You think someone stole my painting?" Now I felt worried —and sick.

"I cannot say that with certainty, but when I arrived this morning to see to the packing and delivery, it was gone from its place on the wall. The security cameras show nothing. The sheriff has been called, of course, but he has no information as yet. If it isn't found, of course a refund will be issued."

I didn't want a refund. I wanted my painting. My heart thumped painfully in my chest—yes, I was a vampire with a heartbeat. The reasons hadn't fully been explained, but Montrose also had a heartbeat, as did a few other vampires, so I never worried about it.

Now, it felt as if my heart were attempting to escape my body, and the pain I was feeling over losing the image of the man—the actual man—that I'd already lost, threatened to overwhelm me.

"We'll keep you updated," the curator said before ending the call. My comp-vid dropped onto my desk when the first tear fell.

Montrose hadn't come to see me in more than two weeks.

He was disappearing from me, too, and I wanted to weep my heart out. Yet here I was, stuck at work with the worst news ever, and no way to do anything about it.

Hastily wiping the wetness from my cheeks, I forced myself into a straighter posture, determined not to think about it.

Until later.

~

Lissa

"Your son," I pointed a food-covered finger in Winkler's direction, "just had a food fight at lunch with his sister."

I knelt next to the bathtub, trying to wrestle Wayne back into the water—he wanted to stand, naked and knee-deep in the water, after kicking half of it out of the tub already.

I was wet, food-covered, and miffed.

"Wayne," Winkler growled.

Wayne went still immediately, then sat down like a two-and-a-half-year-old gentleman waiting to be bathed.

Daddy was the alpha. The alpha was to be obeyed. No wonder werewolf kids stayed with their fathers on Earth, after arranged marriages ended.

"I'll do this," Winkler had walked into my bathroom dressed in nice pants and a white shirt—he'd just come from a meeting on Harifa Edus. Kneeling on the wet floor, he didn't even bother rolling back his shirt sleeves before cleaning Wayne up.

Wayne knew he was in trouble when Daddy got *that* look on his face.

"I take it Sandra is seeing to Wynter?"

"Yeah. I'll go check on them now."

As I walked out of my bathroom, I heard Winkler tell Wayne in a stern voice that food was not to be played with.

"That's an uh, interesting fashion choice," Grant informed me as I walked out of my suite, still covered in mashed peas and potatoes.

"What's wrong?" I studied my clothes for a moment before deciding that if I wanted to ever wear them again, I'd have to employ power to clean them.

"Well, the green peas don't go with the brown gravy," Grant studied the stains carefully.

"No, I meant why are you looking for me?"

"We overheard a comp-vid conversation between Renée and the gallery curator."

"What about? She's not trying to return the painting, is she?" Grant handled my finances, so he knew about my subterfuge in paying for the painting.

"No. Seems like the painting has been sort of—misplaced."

"What?"

"Nothing else was taken, but he swears the painting just disappeared off the wall while the gallery was closed."

"How's she taking it?"

"Not well. She thinks she's hiding the tears, but I've heard her sniffling several times."

"Fuck."

"I thought so, too."

"Has Trevor been called?"

"Yes."

"Good. I want to have a chat with him. Find out where he is."

"I'll have that information for you in five minutes."

"Thank you."

"I have no idea how it was done," Trevor told me. He stood inside my private study—at least I'd had time to clear up the food disaster on my clothes before he arrived.

"You think someone with power was involved, don't you?"

"I don't know what else it could be," he shook his head. "Is Erland here? Maybe he can ferret out the underlying source of this theft."

"You believe it really was stolen?"

"I do. I've seen the security vids. One moment it was there on the wall, the next, it was gone."

"Damn. That painting was for Renée."

"I understand that it looks very much like Montrose."

Trevor would know—he'd been an enforcer and then an assassin for the Vampire Council on Earth, and had seen Montrose and the rest of the Council too many times to count.

"That's why she wanted it," I said. "Because it looked like Montrose. Now she's heartbroken."

"This makes it much worse," Trevor sighed.

"It does," I agreed.

"In all my years of knowing him, I've never known him to court any woman. No, he doesn't prefer males," Trevor held up a hand.

"I think I'd know that," I huffed.

"I think you would, too, but that's what I've seen from him. He's polite—courtly, even, but as for giving his affections, I'd say Renée was the closest thing to receiving anything of the sort from him."

"Trevor, we really need to find that painting."

"I don't have any evidence to go on."

"I know. Do we have recorded images of it—the painting? I'd like to take a closer look, if you don't mind."

"I have images—good ones—from the curator. I'll send those to your comp-vid."

"Thank you."

Renée

"Sheriff Trevor?" I blinked when he walked into my tiny office, his tall frame and wide shoulders filling the space much as Montrose did when he visited.

As he might never again, I reminded myself.

"I just wanted to drop by and tell you we're doing everything we can to recover your stolen property."

"You think it really was stolen?"

"I do. We just don't have any evidence—or solid suspects or leads for that matter, but we're looking into all the gallery visitors who expressed an interest in the work."

"Thank you," I dropped my eyes to study the top of my desk. I felt like crying again, and needed to cut off the tears before they fell.

"Don't worry," he said gently. "If it can be found, we'll find it."

I nodded instead of speaking—if I spoke, my voice would betray just how upset I was, and I worried the information would find its way to Montrose, who'd then look into the matter and discover that I'd bought a painting that looked exactly like him.

I didn't want to be embarrassed further, especially as he was making it obvious that his work as my sire was over and he was gradually disappearing from my life.

Weaning me away, I told myself and sniffled before I could force back the emotion.

"There, now," Trevor handed me a tissue to wipe my nose. "We're doing everything we can to get him back for you."

I nodded again; Trevor left before the floodgates opened.

∾

Montrose

Two days before Christmas, and still there was snow on the ground, with more coming on Christmas Eve.

My mind was filled with memories whenever I looked out my windows, ever since the first fall nearly two weeks earlier.

Too, I'd heard rumors that Renée was troubled about something, and on any other day, during any other season, I'd look into it.

Not now. Not with these painful memories so close—as if they threatened to overwhelm me at any moment. I'd not felt this morose in centuries, and wondered why those recollections were affecting me so badly now—when I was worlds away from the place and time of their creation.

I'd visited the plain below the mountain—the *prats dels cremats*, or *field of the burned* in the Occitan language, where a stele was erected in more modern times.

The stele commemorated more than two hundred lives; lives snuffed out in the flames of politics, combined with the misshapen goals of a more powerful religion.

Als catars, als martirs del pur amor crestian, 16 de març 1244, it reads, meaning *The Cathars, martyrs of pure Christian love*, followed by the date of their deaths, also in the Occitan language.

She was one of them—lying down upon the pyre willingly, and giving up her life after the castle fell to the attackers.

If I'd returned from my mission, would she have agreed to stay with me and leave the fortress together, to find lives elsewhere? The attackers only burned those who refused to renounce their faith.

Burned alive.

What a horrible way to die.

∾

Lissa

"Of course you can go home, sweetheart," I told Renée. She'd been crying again, and I felt like finding Montrose and kicking his tight vampire behind.

He should be here for her. She shouldn't be afraid to contact him when she was this upset, and frankly, he should run (instead of walking or driving, because a vampire running would be faster than both), to the palace and help with this situation.

I waited until Renée, sniffling softly, left my office before I pulled up the images Trevor sent me of the stolen artwork.

The painting was lifelike and accurate—down to the crusted mud drying on the man's boots. Lynx had gone to a lot of trouble to present the image as he had—a man—Montrose—dressed in medieval garb, staring down a snowy, steep mountain as if it were a gauntlet to be run.

Yes, my curiosity was up, and on another day I might have looked into the matter, or placed a few well-intentioned questions. Instead, I decided to wait for the answers to unfold on their own.

Again, I surmised that something or someone was at work, here, and who was I to interfere?

∾

Renée

The home I'd been given, once I completed my five years of

vampire training, was a far cry from the opulence that Montrose inhabited, but it was nice. I only used the second bedroom to store extra clothes—it currently held my summer wardrobe, as Lissia was in the winter season.

Stamping snow off my shoes as I arrived at the front door, I pressed my palm against the pad to release the lock. Here, Weff didn't greet me when I entered—I hadn't seen the comesula since I'd last been inside Montrose's mansion, months ago.

Montrose, as a member of the Queen's Council, warranted a loftier abode, as he often referred to it. Usually he waved off the grandeur, saying it was expected and for show only, as he could be happy living more austerely than was expected of someone of his status.

I'd enjoyed the comforts of it, if I were honest. Having comesuli to clean, cook and wait on us? That had been a wonderful luxury. Montrose, on the other hand, often waved away offers of help and did for himself.

You left work to stop thinking about him, I reminded myself, walking through the front door and hanging my coat on a peg just inside.

Door locked, the lock-bot informed me as I strode toward the kitchen. Maybe eating something would help me out of my funk.

"There's nothing to eat," I sighed, my arm resting on the lower door while I stared at a nearly-empty cold-keeper. I should have gone to the grocers the day before, but news of the missing painting had knocked me off my regular schedule.

I'd either have to go now, or eat out.

Well, I'll get a refund on the painting, I considered, shutting the cold-keeper door and walking out of the kitchen. I could afford something at New Fangled, for certain. Then, I could go to the grocer's afterward, and stock up on necessities.

Maybe you should take a cooking class, a small voice informed me. My skills were limited, still, because most of my life I'd been too sick to learn, and then five years living with Montrose had others doing it for me.

My zap oven had become my best friend after I moved out.

I won't go to New Fangled after all, I decided. There was a sandwich shop next door to Niff's, and Niff's cookies were calling my name.

Yes. That was exactly what I needed.

Sugar.

Sugar—bad idea. I was ready to climb the walls instead of sleeping, and as I was vampire, climbing walls wasn't as far-fetched as most people believed.

I'd bought a dozen cookies, took them home and eaten half the box —after I'd had a sandwich and fries before that.

I found a message on my comp-vid, too, when I got home—a message from Queen Lissa, saying that I didn't have to come in the following day if I didn't want to—she was letting the others off at lunchtime anyway.

I had a few things to finish, so I'd force myself to work half a day— after missing half a day already, sniffling and crying.

Besides, I'd found a gift for Lissa, and I wanted her to have it on the proper day. I had images of her babies that I'd taken with my comp-vid, and I'd found a frame for them. They were adorable, and in the photos I had, looked almost angelic, smiling as I'd caught them playing in Lissa's study.

She needed this—a reminder that they'd grow out of a destructive phase—or so I hoped. I realized I needed friends other than the ones I had at work—neither Grant nor Heathe would appreciate being contacted after midnight because I couldn't sleep.

Montrose might be awake.

He often was, late into the night.

No. I'd gone and eaten sugar to forget him.

Wait—my mind wasn't exactly lucid.

Go to bed and count sheep.

Why did I eat all those cookies?

Montrose

Snow—quite heavy at times, was falling when I rose early—too early, I think, on Christmas Eve.

As Earth measured it.

To most of Le-Ath Veronis, it was just another day. Go to work. Come home. Eat, sleep, do it again tomorrow.

The next Council meeting was scheduled the following week. I had nothing to occupy my time, today.

I should have contacted Renée yesterday, I castigated myself. She was upset about something; Oluwa said so. He'd heard the comesuli gossiping at the palace when he went to visit Cheedas, whom he saw regularly.

Cheedas was his natural, vampire child. Renée was my adopted child, initially turned by the Queen, because males seldom were able to turn females who weren't comesuli to begin with. The Queen's blood was special, and she held the unusual ability to turn a humanoid female, when a male's blood would fail most of the time.

Renée is a special case, she'd told me. I wondered why then, and I still wonder about it, as no explanation was ever given.

"Is this the day?" Weff wandered in, bringing me a cup of tea and a light breakfast.

"The day for what?" I turned to frown at him.

"To open the gift on your desk."

"That," I waved a hand dismissively. "Put the tray on the table by the window, here. I'm watching the snow."

"It's amazing," Weff said. "I noticed just this morning that a neighbor a block over is building what he called *snow men*. They didn't look like any men I've seen, but he was enjoying himself."

I may have mumbled something about vampires who'd never grown out of their childhood. If Weff heard me, he never remarked on it; I only heard the door shut softly as he left my study.

Feeling a moment of remorse, I lifted the cup of tea he'd poured for me and sipped, while continuing to watch the snow. When I next looked down at the table, to decide whether I wanted to eat this early, I found the small, gold bag sitting there beside my covered plate.

Had Weff done this, after I'd waved him off the subject?

Get it over with, my conscience prodded. Setting my tea down, I opened the bag. "What's this?" I grumbled as I lifted a photograph from the bag—that's all it contained. I blinked as my world reversed and sped backward, to a time I'd refused to recall—for centuries.

Renée

"Good morning, Renée," the guard at the side entrance greeted me as I trudged beneath the porte cochère, pausing to stomp snow off my boots. I actually had a pair—Montrose had bought them for me early in my training, when it snowed once before.

They'd stayed in my closet most of the time since, because it seldom snowed and if it did, it never lasted very long.

This time, it had stayed, snowed again and stayed again. For two weeks. An unusual weather pattern, the weather experts all said.

"Short day today," the guard grinned as he held the door open for me.

I considered my lack of sleep and merely nodded at his words.

"Queen Lissa asked for tea," a comesula informed me as I walked through the palace kitchen. "Would you mind taking the tray?"

"Of course not." I often took the tray to her—it saved a kitchen employee from making a useless trip and got the tea to her faster. I usually got a cup, too, and if there were ever a day when I needed the caffeine, it was today.

Setting the Queen's small gift on the tray, I lifted it and walked toward her private study.

Montrose

At first, I thought it was a memory—until the bitter cold and wet snow struck exposed skin and I shivered.

I wasn't dressed for winter on Montsegur—that was certain, and I pulled back, hiding behind a tree when they came walking down the steep, narrow trail.

I knew them.

Knew all of them, from Anton, the knight at the front, to Anselme —and me—at the rear.

I watched my former self, right hand settled on my sword pommel and watchful as we made our way as swiftly as possible down the mountain. I stiffened when I heard a foot slide on loose rock, before a hand from behind the stumbling *perfect* reached out to steady him.

How was I here? Was it a hallucination?

Where had the photograph come from? It depicted this place flawlessly, and I'd fallen through it, like a fictional character in an implausible story.

That's when I remembered. We had almost reached the place— where we'd been attacked.

"No," I whispered, leaving the safety of my hiding place behind and rushing after the fleeing party.

Time slowed. As a vampire, I should have reached the others in a blink, yet my steps felt weighted with enough lead to stop a planet from spinning.

My plan was simple. Fight off the attackers, then return to my love. Was this a chance to get back to her—to prevent a terrible death from happening?

I cannot say.

Their time passed—mine did not.

By the time I arrived on the scene, it was to find Anselme dead and my former self wounded to the point of death. Our attackers had then rushed down the mountain, chasing after the others to obtain the treasure they carried.

I never learned whether they were successful.

A crunch sounded on the trail, diverting my attention. I never knew how swiftly my vampire sire arrived, I only know that he came to me before I expired that night.

He arrived quickly, I learned, and likely heard the battle taking place moments before. It had drawn him like any predator to a meal.

I watched as he considered his options; he could take the last of my living blood and leave me dead, or return some of his own and make a child. He hesitated for longer than I imagined he would, until I groaned *her* name.

Twice.

I hadn't remembered her name—until now. It hit me like the weight of a boulder from the mountain above my head, and I dropped soundlessly to my knees with the joy and pain of it.

"You will not remember her name or her face," my sire placed compulsion upon my dying former self, and set about making the turn.

CHAPTER 3

R enée

"Sit down and have a cup of tea with me, while I open this." Queen Lissa was full of smiles this morning—it was almost Christmas, after all, and she held the small, wrapped gift I'd given her in her hands.

"All right." I settled on the closest chair and lifted the teapot to pour a cup while she carefully unwrapped the gift.

"Ah," she smiled when she opened the double frame to reveal the photographs inside. "Oh, my gosh, this is so perfect," she held the frame against her breast with one hand and wiped tears away with the other. "This will stay here," she set the frame on a corner of her desk, so she could see it whenever she sat there.

"They're sweet," I said after taking a sip of my tea. "They just have a lot of energy to expend every day."

Lissa's indrawn breath made me lift my eyes to hers. "You're right," she whispered. "We need to find structured activities for them, to wear them out." She began sorting through her desk drawer for a comp-vid.

While today and tomorrow might be a holiday for the Queen of Le-Ath Veronis, it was just another day on Le-Ath Veronis as a whole.

"I'll get Sandra to help with this," Lissa muttered, searching her comp-vid for games and toys designed for physical activity. "Do you think they're too young to take swimming lessons?"

"I don't think anyone is too young for that," I smiled at her.

"Perfect. I'll pay for swimming lessons, and then kickball lessons, and more lessons after that. They're quite agile for their age."

"Yes, they are," I agreed. "Just don't forget to make it fun. Perhaps arrange for playdates with other ah, similar children."

"Another excellent idea. I'll see to it." Lissa continued to search through her comp-vid.

"Well, I have things to do," I yawned when I stood. "Let me know if I can help in any way."

Lissa half-waved at me as I left her study behind, heading for my much smaller office. Waving on the lights, I entered, only to stop dead in my tracks.

The painting hung on the back wall of my small space, covering most of the wall with its imposing presence. A white envelope was lodged in the lower left corner, with my name written on it.

I ignored the envelope, sighing over the image of Montrose in the painting. It had to be him—it was exactly like him. And, since he'd stopped coming to visit, I could keep it here and he'd never know.

Sheriff Trevor must have tracked down the thief, I thought as I stepped forward to retrieve the envelope.

It wasn't a note from Trevor. Or from any other law enforcement agency. The note was from the artist himself.

Dear Renée, the note began, *I wanted you to know the name of the man in this painting. Not the name he uses now, but his full name: Philippe David de Toulouse, Knight-Protector. Montrose is only a name which means "Mountain Rose," and is derived from the French language on old Earth.*

You see, he couldn't remember her name, so he called her—and himself—what he knew of her; Montrose. After all, one didn't name oneself after his favorite title for her; Ma Rose des Pics.

Sincerely, Lynx.

Her? Who was she? Was he in love with another woman? I

crumpled the note in my hands before dropping to my knees to weep beneath his portrait.

~

Lissa

Grant stood in my office, watching me ooh and ahh over the new sunglasses case he'd gotten me for Christmas, when we heard it.

"That sounds like Montrose yelling," Grant frowned and turned toward the door. "Can't be," he added. "Montrose is far too proper to yell anything at anybody."

"Wait," I said, setting the case aside and standing. "He *is* yelling. That's Montrose. Oh, my gosh, he's yelling Renée's name."

By the sound of things, he was running through my palace while yelling for her, too. "Come on," I grabbed Grant's hand and pulled him out my door. "We have to see this."

~

Renée

I was sobbing; therefore, I didn't hear it at first. Someone was yelling inside the palace, making marble halls and walls echo with the sound, distorting it.

Until it came closer.

I sobbed again when I imagined it was Montrose shouting my name—as if his life depended upon it. That, of course, was wishful thinking in the extreme. Montrose never yelled—at anything or anybody. It was beneath his dignity.

I jerked when my desk was upended and thrown against the adjacent wall, crashing through it as if it were tissue paper torn through.

There I was, tear-stains and all, on my knees beneath a portrait of Montrose, when I cowered beneath my attacker—only to discover it was Montrose himself.

Had he learned about the painting, and come to chastise me over it?

That was the only thought I had time to think before he was on his knees beside me, wrapping me in his arms so tightly I couldn't breathe, and whispering words against my hair.

Words I didn't recognize, except for these; *ma rose des pics, I have waited so long for you to return to me.*

I had no idea what all of it meant, but it was said with such care—and—love, perhaps? It didn't matter—I was in his arms and wept tears of joy.

~

Lissa

"I'd say he remembered." Breanne appeared at my elbow as Grant and I watched the scene unfold before us.

Now I knew who was behind this—but I'd suspected all along. After all, Breanne was the one who'd asked me to turn Renée to begin with. The Mighty Heart never asks for favors—unless there is something that is required—a need to be fulfilled.

"Come away," she urged after a few more seconds passed. "They need alone time, and you need to give her a leave of absence. Montrose should take her to do all the things she's never gotten to do before."

With one more look at the couple on their knees inside Renée's office, I walked back to my study with Bree and Grant. I'm sure I'd find out the details later.

Yes. I definitely would.

~

Montrose

"My love." I almost couldn't bear to hold her away from me, but we needed to talk. To say things to one another.

And I needed to apologize.

"Is this true?" Renée's eyes were red from weeping, and she'd never been more beautiful to me.

"It is true, *ma rose*. More than true."

"What do those words mean?" she asked. "*Ma rose des pics?*"

"Ah. It is French, my native language," I admitted. "It translates to *my rose of the peaks*. It comes from a particular mountain in southern France on Earth, a peak near other peaks in the Pyrenees."

"How did this happen?" she asked as another tear slipped down her cheek. I reached out to wipe it away with a thumb.

"Oh, my love," I pulled her against me again. "I have loved you all my life. I merely forgot it for a while. Please forgive me."

"Will you kiss me?"

"Of course I will. As many times as you want, and more, too."

"Do you still want to be called Montrose? Or do you want me to call you Philippe?" she asked after I'd kissed her—several times.

I pulled away this time. "Where did you learn that name?" I looked at her sternly. She shrank away.

"No, love, never do that," I sighed, standing and pulling her to her feet so I could hold her better.

"The artist knew your name. I don't know how," she said, her voice trembling.

"Artist?"

"Of the painting. He painted you, Montrose. It's why I bought it." She turned in my arms to point out a rather large painting hanging on her wall. I stared at it—as did she, only she gasped.

"That's not—the painting I bought. Or the one that was here earlier," she breathed.

"What? What do you mean?" I asked. I couldn't take my eyes away from it. It depicted a couple.

That couple—Renée and I—stood atop a stone outcropping on Montsegur. The two of us, together, easily recognizable as ourselves, as I gave a mountain flower to my love that day. It was the day I'd first told her of my love for her, and it would always stay in my memory.

"I wasn't in the painting—not the one I bought. It was only you, I swear," Renée breathed.

"You do not like this?"

"I love it. But—how?"

"*Mon amour*, I believe greater things are happening than we can ever fathom. Until today, those things only happened to others. This is our miracle, I think. Our Christmas miracle. Now, answer me if you can; will you marry me?"

Six months later

Lissa

"I can't believe this," Grant fished for the olive in his drink. He didn't like Champagne, so he'd asked for a martini.

"Believe what?"

"That they'd dress like the couple in that painting."

"I think it's awesome."

"But her dress is so plain. I'd like to see her really gussied up."

"Honey, you'll probably see that at the next ball thrown by the Council," I sniffed. "This is their day, and that's what they wanted."

"Hey," Winkler sidled up to me and kissed my cheek.

"Where have you been?" I lifted an eyebrow.

"Supervising the kids' swimming lessons. I think they can win the Olympics next year."

"Honey, you know we don't have the Olympics in the Alliances."

"But they'd win if we did."

"Then you'd better start looking for a college with a swim team," I said. "Vamp U doesn't have an athletics program."

"Yet," Winkler grinned.

"Aww—they're kissing again," Grant breathed, making Winkler and me turn our heads toward the newly-married couple.

"Just as it should be," Lynx appeared, a wide grin on his face.

"Who all was involved in this subterfuge?" I poked him in the ribs.

"Oh, let's see. Bree, Conner, Trevor, Ashe, Zaria—a bunch of people, actually. I only did the paintings; I don't have the full story."

"Right. I'll get to the bottom of this if it's the last thing I do."

"Then ask your sister. I think she'll give you the scoop. By the way, the first painting is a wedding gift that will be delivered later —anonymously."

"Fine."

"Fine," he countered and walked away, heading for the serving table and a very tall cake, pieces of which were being handed out to anyone and everyone.

"I don't think anybody was ever charged for those paintings—either of them," I observed.

"It's a miracle," Winkler laughed.

And so it was.

The End

www.ingramcontent.com/pod-product-compliance
Lightning Source LLC
Chambersburg PA
CBHW071005120726
47910CB00004B/1398